Dear Reader,

I've always love..
called to ask if I...................... ...... BABY BOOM
series, I didn't have to think long before saying yes!
Besides, I had my very own research institute
operating—my three grandchildren who, at the ages
of four, three and one, were already keeping track of
whose turn it was to stay with Grandpa and Grandma.

The two boys provided Sam's gorgeous dark eyes
and curly blond hair, and baby Ashley was a wealth
of cute tricks and a first-class education in nonverbal
communication—just Sam's style. In fact, she even
modeled for the cover artist, so he could get the
kitchen-sink bathtub just right.

I hope you'll enjoy meeting Sam as much as I
enjoyed creating him. Oh, and I hope you'll like
watching Kady and Devlin fall in love, too!

Love,

Leigh Michaels

P.S. I like hearing from readers. You can write to me
at P.O. Box 935, Ottumwa, Iowa, 52501-0935

BABY
BOOM

Leigh Michaels has written over fifty books for Harlequin, and continues to be a much-loved, bestselling author all around the world. Four of Leigh's novels have been nominated for RITA Awards, and critics have praised her warmly:

Of *The Only Solution*:

"An interesting dilemma, strong characters and a little baby make THE ONLY SOLUTION a wonderful romance. Michaels writes with a depth of feeling that adds a gentle dimension."

—*Affaire de Coeur*

Of *Invitation To Love*:

"Fascinating characters overcoming insurmountable odds are only part of what will have you eagerly turning the pages to Leigh Michaels' latest."

—*Romantic Times*

Of *The Daddy Trap*:

"Leigh Michaels develops an interesting conflict."

—*Romantic Times*

Of *The Only Man for Maggie*:

"Leigh Michaels really makes the sparks fly as this attractive couple search for just the right compromise in this endearing tale brimming with piquant dialogue and a stimulating conflict."

—*Romantic Times*

Look out for *The Fake Fiancé!* in October (#3478), the lively follow-up to Leigh Michaels's 50th book, *The Perfect Divorce!*

Baby, You're Mine!
Leigh Michaels

Harlequin Books

TORONTO • NEW YORK • LONDON
AMSTERDAM • PARIS • SYDNEY • HAMBURG
STOCKHOLM • ATHENS • TOKYO • MILAN
MADRID • WARSAW • BUDAPEST • AUCKLAND

For my research team:
Train Brain, who contributed Sam's dark eyes
Alexander the Great,
who let Sam borrow his curly blond hair
and Little Miss Muffin,
who invented all of Sam's cutest tricks—
With love, Grandma

ISBN 0-373-03463-6

BABY, YOU'RE MINE!

First North American Publication 1997.

Copyright © 1997 by Leigh Michaels.

Printed in U.S.A.

CHAPTER ONE

THE hum of Kady Bishop's laptop computer mingled with the growl of the refrigerator's compressor, creating an unpleasant drone that rasped on her eardrums and made it difficult to concentrate. She stared at the screen, which demanded to know if she was ready for the computer to process all the information she'd entered, and hesitated. Was she *positive* she'd plugged in all the numbers?

Of course she had, she told herself irritably. Doing a payroll was child's play, really. The problem was that she simply had to learn to focus her attention in the midst of hubbub. There wasn't any choice, if she was going to keep this client.

Down the stairs from the main level of the town house floated a tinkling laugh, which scratched Kady's nerves like fingernails on a blackboard. Shelle Emerson laughed that way only when the boss was around, and Kady had never been certain whether it was the laugh itself or the fact that it meant Devlin Cunningham was nearby that exasperated her so.

Of course, she thought irritably, it was about time he came to life. It was past four in the afternoon!

She punched the button that set the computer program in motion just as a lanky young man in cutoff jeans appeared in the kitchen doorway.

He eyed Kady over the top of his dark-framed glasses. "Are the paychecks ready yet?"

"They'll start printing in a minute, Hal, as soon as the computer processes all the deductions."

"You've been ages getting them done today."

"It's hard to concentrate on a payroll when everyone keeps interrupting me."

"Well, if you insist on setting up your office in the kitchen, you can't expect us all to stay away from you. Especially when it's this hot." Hal opened the refrigerator door and stood staring at the shelves—as if, Kady thought, he was basking in the cool air.

She stood it as long as she could before saying, "Would you please shut that door? If you can't find what you want within thirty seconds, it's probably not there at all."

He took a can of diet soda from the top shelf and popped it open. "Touchy today, aren't we?"

"A bit, I suppose," Kady admitted. "That refrigerator hums at a pitch that makes my ears hurt, and the longer the door's open, the longer the motor runs."

He shrugged. "Then don't camp in the kitchen."

"Where else do you suggest I work? There's nowhere in this madhouse with enough clear space to set up a laptop except the kitchen table." The computer beeped, and Kady turned on the tiny printer and fed in a sheet of checks.

Hal perched on the corner of the table. "You can't blame everybody for being especially anxious to get their money. As soon as I have that check, I'm out of here for the next four days. So if you want to get rid of me—"

Kady looked up. "I didn't say I wanted to get rid of you. Maybe I have plans for the long weekend, too, and I'm just as anxious to get out of here as you are."

He stared at her thoughtfully with a shadow of doubt in his eyes.

Kady sighed inwardly. Did she really look like a

woman who couldn't possibly have plans for an exciting long holiday weekend?

Shelle's tinkling laugh sounded again, from the stairway this time.

"Now there's a woman with plans," Hal murmured.

Kady's eyebrows rose a fraction. Obviously she wasn't the only one who'd noticed that Shelle laughed in that particular way only when Devlin Cunningham was within earshot.

"If I was the boss," Hal went on, "I'd watch out for that lady."

"But then," Kady said crisply, "perhaps you have more common sense than he does." She fed another sheet of checks into the printer, looked over the finished ones and tore off the serrated margins. "Here, Hal. Enjoy your weekend."

Hal glanced at the check, folded it neatly and slid it into his wallet. "Oh, I'm planning to. I love it when the Fourth of July falls on Tuesday so we get a really long weekend. We're having a three-day beer bust at my buddy's house out on the North Shore. His parents have a private beach and everything. If you want to come, I'll give you the address."

"It's thoughtful of you—but no, thanks."

"Right," Hal scoffed. "You have plans. What are you going to do, anyway? Reprogram your computer? Or read the tax code, maybe? That's no way to spend a long, hot summer weekend."

Kady didn't bother to answer. Hal would never understand the satisfaction she expected to find in getting another hundred proposals ready to mail to prospective clients and then sinking into a tub of warm bubbles with a novel to relax after the work was done.

Besides, Hal didn't wait for an answer. "I think I hear the boss coming," he said. "You haven't seen me, all right?"

Before Kady could point out that the absence of his payroll check from the stack would certainly give him away without her saying anything at all, Hal had slid out the back door and up the steps from the basement kitchen to the courtyard. She saw his shadow flit past the window just as Shelle Emerson came in.

"I think we should have a glass of wine to celebrate," Shelle said, and gave a flip to her long red hair.

The gesture was far too casual to be unplanned, Kady thought. She tried to focus her attention on Shelle, noting the length of her skirt—it would have been indecently short on any woman who carried an ounce more flesh than Shelle did—and her perfect makeup. But her survey of the other woman was mechanical, and in mere seconds Kady found her gaze sliding to the man standing just behind Shelle.

She was annoyed with herself. Why couldn't she simply ignore him?

Because he's a client, she reminded herself. A darned important one, too, at least until she got her practice off the ground and could afford to pick and choose. *And even if he wasn't...*

Kady stopped that thought in its tracks. Devlin Cunningham could be—all right, she admitted, he *was*—stunningly good-looking, in a careless sort of way. Even in threadbare jeans and a half-buttoned, wrinkled shirt, with his dark gold hair rumpled and what looked like a couple of days' growth of beard, he was downright easy on the eyes.

If, Kady reminded herself, you liked that sort of thing—which she emphatically did not. She straightened the already perfect lapel of her cream-colored linen jacket and fed another sheet of checks into the printer.

Shelle took a bottle of wine from the refrigerator and started to rummage through the cupboards, apparently trying to find two stemmed glasses among the polyglot assortment.

Kady watched her for a moment and then said under her breath, "I'd think orange juice would be more appropriate."

Devlin's eyes narrowed. "Why?"

Just one low, soft word, but the richness of his voice seemed to encircle Kady like a summer cloud. Did the man have the hearing of a jungle cat? She felt her cheeks coloring—only because she hadn't intended to make her thoughts public, she told herself. But it was too late to back out now, so she lifted her chin and said, "Considering that you've only just gotten up..."

He grinned, and golden flecks sprang to life in his dark eyes. "Does that mean you're offering to cook me breakfast?"

The tone of his voice, Kady thought, made it sound as if he was inviting her to join him in bed instead. "Hardly," she snapped.

Shelle's laugh trilled. "Don't be silly, Dev, darling. Kady—like most accountants—is only useful for cooking the books." She found a corkscrew in the tool drawer and brandished it. "Will you open the wine, Devlin? You're so much better at it than I am."

He took the corkscrew, but he hardly glanced at it. "Sorry, Shelle, but I don't have time for a glass of wine right now. Run along, will you? I need to talk to Kady."

The playful, seductive note was gone from his voice, Kady noted, and she wondered with a twinge of panic what on earth had happened. Surely he wasn't unhappy with the accounting service she'd provided for the past six months. She'd worked her tail off to get his financial affairs organized.

Shelle pouted. "Only if you promise me a real celebration later. I'm going to be in town this weekend."

"Will you?" Devlin asked absently. "Maybe I'll give

you a call." He pulled a chair around and straddled it, folding his arms across the back.

Kady felt her fingers trembling as she fed yet another sheet of checks into the printer. There was something about the way he was looking at her.... She fumbled through the finished stack, found Shelle's name and tore her check out of the sheet. "Here, Shelle. I assume you'd like this before you leave?"

Shelle took it and flounced out. Devlin didn't seem to notice. He was still studying Kady.

His gaze felt warm—as if he was directing an energy field at her skin. Kady sat up a little straighter and primly tugged the hem of her slim skirt down to her knees.

Devlin smiled. "That's very sexy, you know."

"What?"

"Drawing attention to a perfect set of legs by pulling on your skirt that way."

She swallowed hard. "What was it you wanted to talk to me about, Devlin?"

His gaze slid slowly from her hemline to her almost black hair, twisted in a knot atop her head. "Am I making you nervous, Kady?"

"No," Kady lied. "I absolutely love being stared at by a wolf. It's the biggest pleasure I've experienced in the six months I've been doing your accounting."

He smiled. "Did my grandmother tell you I was a wolf before she sent you over to talk to me about my bookkeeping?"

Kady was honestly startled. "Of course not. She told me your financial affairs were in a mess—which they were—and that you were spending your trust fund at a rate only slightly less than the speed of light—which you still are. Other than that, she didn't say much at all."

Devlin looked thoughtful. "Honestly? I thought that kind of warning might be why you'd been playing the role of hard-to-get virgin since the day you first showed up.''

Kady gritted her teeth. "For your information, I haven't been playing any role at all.''

"This is the real you?" He shook his head sadly. "Well, don't take your bedroom problems out on me, Kady.''

"I don't have any bedroom problems!''

Devlin smiled. "Or any adventure, either, obviously. That's a pity.''

Kady took a deep breath and tried to relax. She'd risen to the bait before she'd paused to think, and she'd better get a grip fast or things would only get worse.

He surprised her by sobering suddenly. "My grandmother is due back next week from her round-the-world trek.''

"I know. She faxed me yesterday to tell me to meet her plane at O'Hare on Tuesday. Where she found a fax machine in Uganda is beyond me, but...''

"She was in Uganda? I wonder what she was doing there.'' He considered for a moment and shook his head. "It's a waste of time to think about it.''

"No doubt—where Iris is concerned. Did she send you here to be a spy?''

Kady frowned. "A spy? What do you mean?''

"I suppose your assignment, as soon as she gets home, is to tell her everything you've discovered about my business.''

"I'm not so sure I'd call this a business," Kady said thoughtfully. "And I'm not so sure Iris would want to know the details, anyway. But I'm positive that I don't like being labeled a spy.''

"Come on—what else would you call it? Even if you didn't agree to the deal up front, if Iris asked, you'd tell her everything you knew. Wouldn't you?''

Kady was silent. It was a difficult call. Devlin was her

client, and professional ethics said she shouldn't breathe a word about his private affairs to anyone. Still, Iris Cunningham wasn't just anyone. She was, in a sense, Kady's client, too.

"What's making you hesitate?" Devlin asked softly.

"Loyalty."

"To me?"

"Are you joking? If it wasn't for your grandmother—" Kady stopped. If Devlin Cunningham didn't already understand why she felt the tug of loyalty for Iris, there was no way to explain it to his satisfaction.

And quite possibly he didn't understand, Kady thought. After all, he'd had everything handed to him from the moment he was born—family, private-school education, trust fund. He was no doubt incapable of understanding the struggle of someone who'd had none of those things.

"I'd say the question is why you're so worried about my intentions," she countered. "Are you planning to do something Iris wouldn't like?"

"What I do isn't any of Iris's business. I just wondered if I should expect her to know all my inside plans just as soon as you do."

Kady shrugged. "What makes you think I haven't told her everything I know already?"

"Because even if you are her favorite little godchild, her communication has been strictly one-way for the last four months. The only thing I've heard from her was an order to have a happy birthday—with no return address. How do you know she was in Uganda yesterday, anyway? Did she say so?"

"No," Kady admitted. "I looked up the phone codes from the number on the fax. And just to set the record straight, I'm not her godchild."

Devlin shrugged. "When you've got a hundred, what's one more or less?"

"Do these inside plans you're so worried about—"

"Who said I was worried?"

Kady waved a hand carelessly. "Have anything to do with Shelle's celebration? What was that all about, anyway?"

"She struck a deal with a publisher to sell me the remainder stock of every new comic book they print."

"Another publisher?" Kady sighed. "Do you really think you need *more* comic books, Devlin?"

"Of course." Devlin sounded faintly surprised that she would even ask. "I'm planning to sell them, you know."

"When? And to whom? If they're remainders, that means they didn't sell the first time they hit the market, so what makes you think—"

"Kady, what's the matter with you? When the time's right—"

"The question is whether I'll be alive to see it."

"You're supposed to pay my bills, Bishop, not critique them."

"Having some income so I can do that wouldn't be a bad plan. But as long as you're selling one comic book for every dozen that come in—"

"Have I told you lately," Devlin said gently, "that I'm so pleased to have you as my chief financial orator? Oh, sorry—I meant chief financial *officer*."

"I refuse to be annoyed by a cheap jab like that." Kady turned off the printer and computer and began to pack everything in her briefcase. "So if you're finished trying to persuade me not to talk to Iris, I'll go distribute the paychecks and get out of your way."

"I wasn't trying to persuade you, just find out what you intend to do."

Kady paused as she unhooked the cable that linked computer and printer. "Oh, really?"

"Really," Devlin assured her, and smiled. "If I ever

decide to start a campaign to persuade you of anything, Kady, believe me—you'll know it.''

He pushed his chair into place and left the room. She heard him go into the room next to the kitchen where most of his comic books were stored, whistling as if he didn't have a care in the world.

Kady shivered, and then told herself not to be an idiot. His threat had been only an idle one. In any case, it was silly to assume it had anything to do with the sizzling way he'd looked at her. That had been purely a matter of habit on his part. There was no shortage of truly beautiful women in Devlin Cunningham's life. Shelle had a lot stronger competition than Kady Bishop could ever hope to provide.

And that was perfectly all right with Kady. There was nothing she needed less than a man who seemed devoted to the twin principles of savoring every gorgeous woman who walked by and owning every comic book ever published. It was a toss-up, Kady thought, which addiction would bankrupt him first.

She left her computer in the kitchen and climbed the stairs to the main level of the town house to hand out the payroll checks. Hal wasn't the only one who had waited impatiently for his money. The staff melted away as Kady passed among the cubicles, and before long the offices were silent and deserted.

Kady took advantage of the opportunity to look around. She'd never really taken the time to look beyond the office atmosphere of the main floor to study how the town house's builders had intended it to look.

What had once been a single large room, a combination of formal living space and dining area, had been carved up with chest-high movable walls into a dozen cubicles. But there was no mistaking the original quality. The town house represented the best of modern design. The room's proportions were soothing, the low stone fireplace along one wall was inviting, and the airy wood and wrought-iron staircase that rose from one side of the room to the floor above—Devlin Cunningham's private quarters—fell just short of being a piece of art in itself.

On a table in what had once been the living room lay a stack of comic books, a dozen or more copies of the same title. Kady glanced at the cover and shook her head. *The Crime Stompers*? That was one she hadn't seen before. What was there about such a subject that had the power to fascinate a grown man—especially a sophisticated sort like Devlin Cunningham?

Kady still wasn't certain why he needed a dozen people to keep track of what he fondly called a business. They all seemed to stay busy, and stacks of comic books appeared to move around the town house and in and out of the mail. But when Kady had asked, soon after she'd started straightening out the tangled finances of Cunningham Enterprises, what all the employees did, Devlin had said simply that he'd make sure they did their work, and her job was only to pay them.

Kady sighed. He was right. It wasn't her responsibility to keep Devlin Cunningham solvent, just to make sure he understood the long-term implications of his financial dealings. And it wasn't up to her to report his business to his grandmother, either, no matter how interested Iris Cunningham might be. Not, of course, that Kady was going to rush to reassure Devlin of that.

Thankfully, with the payroll finished, she had an entire blessed week—the long weekend to work on promoting her business and the following few days to take care of her other clients—before she had to face him again.

She went to the kitchen to pick up her computer and was startled to see Devlin at the refrigerator, pouring orange juice into a tall glass. "It sounded good," he said with a shrug, and downed half the juice in a long gulp.

"Are you going to the Fourth of July picnic at the orphanage this weekend?"

"Why do you want to know?" Kady asked warily.

"You're a deadly suspicious sort, aren't you? Iris
stuck me with the job of emceeing the program, so I was
just wondering if you'd managed to escape—and if so,
how you pulled it off."

Kady sighed. "No. I'm refereeing the games."

"My sympathies."

"I don't mind at all—it's a good cause, and I go every
year anyway. But Oakwood School isn't an orphanage,
you know, and if you're wise, you won't call it that from
the speakers' platform."

Devlin shrugged. "Whatever."

Kady persisted, "It's a group home for troubled and
disadvantaged youth."

"Which were you?"

"I beg your pardon?"

"Were you troubled or disadvantaged? And how long
were you there?"

She hadn't realized that Iris must have told him about
her background. "Disadvantaged," she said crisply.
"And I came there when I was nine and stayed till I
was eighteen. Anything else you'd like to know?"

"So for you the picnic is like going home?"

"Well—not exactly. But it wasn't a bad place to grow
up. It certainly beat the alternatives. And I like going to
the picnic."

"Good for you. I'm not looking forward to it."

Kady shrugged. "You could always liven things up
by taking Shelle, I suppose."

The doorbell rang, chiming the first seven notes of
Haydn's *Surprise Symphony.*

"I've got to change that damned bell," Devlin muttered. He drained the rest of his orange juice. "Somehow
I don't think the orphanage picnic is the kind of cele-

bration Shelle had in mind. Anyway, I didn't mean I was opposed to going. I just don't like the idea of being master of ceremonies. Tell you what, Kady—I'll trade you jobs. You emcee, and I'll run the games.''

"I'll think about it. Aren't you going to answer the door?''

"Why should I?'' He put his empty glass into the sink and stretched lazily, like a cat. "Everybody but you has gone for the weekend. Besides, they all use the back door—so it's not an employee who's been locked out. I haven't ordered pizza, I don't want to talk to salesmen, and it's far too late in the day for the paperboy to be delivering.''

"If you answered it, you wouldn't have to listen to the music any more.''

"You call that music?'' He opened the refrigerator door. "Why is there nothing in here but yogurt? I wonder what happened to all the eggs.''

"Why ask me? If you insist on running your house like a commune and letting a dozen employees have the full run of your kitchen, you shouldn't be surprised at anything you lose. See you at the picnic.''

She didn't wait for an answer, but walked through the lower level and up the stairs toward the front door. The regular employees might use the back entrance, but the only parking spot Kady had been able to find this afternoon was on the street, and she didn't feel like walking all the way around the complex to get to her car.

The bell didn't peal again, and by the time Kady reached the front door she'd forgotten about it and was planning the direct-mail letter she wanted to send to prospective clients. She pulled the door open, turned to make sure the spring lock was set and walked almost straight into the man on the front step.

"Delivery for Mr. Cunningham,'' he said.

Kady blinked. "I don't think he's expecting anything."

The man grinned. "No," he agreed. "I'd say, myself, that the expecting part was—oh, some time ago."

What on earth was the man rambling about? Kady looked more closely at the bulky bundle in his arms, then at the taxi that was double-parked, motor idling, in front of the town house.

The taxi driver thrust the awkward package at her, and automatically Kady took it. The unexpected weight, combined with her unwieldy computer case, almost tipped her over, and by the time she'd regained her balance the man had touched two fingers to his cap and hurried to the cab.

"Wait a minute!" she called, but he'd already slid behind the wheel, and an instant later the cab roared off in a cloud of blue smoke.

From under a lightweight cloth draping the bundle in her arms, a whimper sounded.

A puppy, Kady thought frantically. But she knew better. The awkward, padded framework she held wasn't an ordinary box or even a pet kennel, but an infant's car seat.

Cautiously, as if she might be revealing a bomb, she pulled the cloth back. Under a friz of curly flaxen hair, wide eyes stared unblinkingly at her from a round baby face.

Dark brown eyes.

Eyes, she thought, just like Devlin's.

She took the stairs to the lower level at a dead run and pulled up just inside the kitchen, out of breath not from exertion but from shock.

Devlin was watching a bag of popcorn rotate in the microwave. "What's after you? You sounded like a whole herd of..." He paused. "What's that you've got?"

Kady's tongue felt thick. "It's a baby."

"A baby what? Where'd you get it?"

"A baby *baby*," she said desperately. "A taxi driver dropped it off."

Devlin's eyebrows arched. "Is it yours?"

"Of course not!"

"Then obviously he made a mistake. Call the cab company and have him come back and get it."

"I didn't get the number of the cab."

"They'll track him down. Or call the orphanage—that's what they're for. They'll sort out who it belongs to."

"I told you, Oakwood isn't an orphanage. Besides, the taxi driver asked for you."

"Me? Whatever for?"

Kady set the seat down in the middle of the table, and the lightweight blanket slid to the floor. "There's a note, too," she said with relief, and pointed to the child's chest. Pinned to the exact center of the pale yellow T-shirt was an envelope, with Devlin's name and the address of the town house on the front.

The baby's face screwed up into a grimace, and it waved its arms wildly.

Devlin peered over her shoulder. "What does the note say?"

"You don't think *I'm* going to open it, do you? It's not addressed to me."

"I doubt it'll bite. Though I suppose the kid might, if we get too close." He unpinned the envelope and tore it open.

Kady watched his face. It was an interesting phenomenon, watching him turn almost purple, then chalk white. She wondered if green would be next. Fascinating. One would think the man had never considered the idea of a child being dumped on him. But surely...

"Well?" she prompted.

"Remember? It isn't addressed to you."

The baby's whimpers escalated into yells, and its face grew red. Almost automatically, Kady unfastened the strap that secured the child in the seat and picked it up. Then she plucked the sheet of cheap notepaper from Devlin's fingers and read it aloud.

"'Devlin—I can't handle this responsibility just now, so it's up to you.'"

"Must you repeat it?" Devlin growled.

Kady raised an eyebrow at him and kept reading. "'I know you don't want him, but he's as much yours as mine.' Well, well, *well*. 'I just hope you'll be more reliable for him than you were for me.' Then there's a signature I can't read, and 'P.S. His name's Sam.' You mean you didn't even know your son's *name*?"

"That," Devlin said, "isn't the half of it."

Automatically, Kady began to shift her weight from one foot to the other in a rocking motion, and the baby nestled into her shoulder and quieted. "What does that mean?"

"It means," Devlin said heavily, "that I can't read the signature, either."

"So? You must know who..." Kady paused.

"I don't have a clue who sent that note. Or the kid."

Kady's jaw dropped. "You mean there have been so many women in your bed that you don't have any idea who the mother of your child is?" Her voice was almost a screech, and the baby started to wail again. Hastily she started to rock once more. "It's okay, Sam," she crooned. "It's okay, baby."

"You don't need to make me sound like Casanova!"

"Hey, don't put the blame on me. You're doing a pretty good job of that without my help." She patted the baby's back. "Poor little Sam."

The baby gave a soft sigh and snuggled his face into her neck.

"I'd say that he likes you. I've got a great idea, Kady—"

"Oh, no," Kady said hastily. "I have my own plans, thank you very much. Good luck, Devlin. I hope you figure out who his mother is, because Sam might want to know someday."

She held the baby out to Devlin—or at any rate, she tried to. One tiny hand seized her earring, the other clutched with a death's grip at her black silk blouse, and a shriek of surprising power almost deafened her.

Devlin folded his arms across his chest. "Sounds a little like a fire engine, doesn't he?" His voice was mild. "He appears to have decided he's yours. And of course you were the first person he saw here. Imprinting—isn't that the term?"

"He's not a bird, Devlin."

"Well, he looks like one, with his mouth open that way, and his face turning red."

The baby wailed and clutched at her hair, at her jacket, at her nose, till Kady gave up and nestled him close once more. Sam buried his face in her shoulder, hiccuped once and was silent.

"So," Devlin said cheerfully, "what were you telling me about your plans?"

Suddenly, Kady felt a little like howling herself.

CHAPTER TWO

WHAT he needed, Devlin thought in desperation, was some time. Time to figure out how his perfectly satisfactory life had suddenly gotten turned upside down. Time to decide what on earth he was going to do about it.

But time to think was the one thing the fates were obviously going to deny him. Caught as he was between a woman with a caustic tongue and an infant boy with lungs the size of Lake Michigan, Devlin might as well wish for the moon as for a little quiet.

And now, he realized with dread, Kady was trying to hand him the kid. He didn't even know how to hold a baby. What was he supposed to do if she walked out and left him with a fuzzy-haired rug rat on his hands?

But Sam obviously had other ideas. Thank heaven the kid had an instinct for self-preservation, Devlin thought, as he watched one tiny hand grab for Kady's earring.

It was funny Devlin hadn't noticed her earrings before. The dangling bits of gold filigree were the most feminine part of her attire.

The infant's other hand clutched Kady's black blouse, tugging at the neckline, and suddenly Devlin found himself looking down at a stunning display of cleavage and the edge of a red lace bra.

Red lace, he thought delightedly. So the prim and proper Miss Bishop had a decidedly romantic streak under that tailored facade! Not that he had either time or energy for thinking about that just now. He guessed he had about three minutes to convince her to stay. And if he didn't succeed...

Well, he wasn't going to waste precious seconds worrying about that just now.

"So, what were you telling me about your plans?" he asked. "Because it looks as if Sam has other ideas."

"Oh, no, you don't, Devlin Cunningham. This baby isn't my problem."

"I'm only going to need a little help, while I get this sorted out. If you'll just—"

"Well, the sorting-out part isn't a bad idea." Kady's voice had an acid edge. "Tell me, do you have a plan for where to start? I mean, do you keep a catalog of the ladies in your life, or will you have to rely entirely on your memory?"

He noted that despite the tone of her voice, Kady was still shifting from one foot to the other, gently rocking the child. Since Sam appeared to be perfectly content in her arms, Devlin decided he'd be wise to ignore the jibe and direct her attention to the baby. "He obviously likes you."

"It's probably just the feminine touch. Or scent, maybe. He doesn't have anything personal against you, Devlin. At this age, babies often have a preference for—"

"What age?"

Kady sighed. "I don't suppose you have any idea of that, either?" She held the child slightly away from her and looked at him. Sam's face wrinkled in protest, and she drew him against her chest. "He's got all eight of his front teeth. I'd say ten, eleven months, maybe a little more. But who am I to guess? I told you, Devlin, I have plans that do not include a baby, so—"

"I'm not asking about the rest of your life," he said irritably. "Just for a few days, till I can figure out what's going on. What's so important, anyway? Are you taking a man to the orphanage picnic Sunday to introduce him to the family?''

Kady looked at him levelly. "You don't need to be sarcastic."

He said hastily, "I didn't intend to be. Honestly. If it's something like that, can't you just call him up and tell him you've had an emergency?"

Kady smiled. It was really a very nice smile, Devlin noted. Her lips were just full enough to be extremely inviting.

"But I haven't," she said gently. "*You're* the one with the emergency, and that's an entirely different thing. There's no reason on earth I should cancel work on my ad campaign in order to bail you out of a jam."

Devlin pounced. "Ad campaign?"

She looked, he thought, as if she'd like to kick herself—or, more likely, him.

"To get new clients," she admitted finally. "I spend so much time on my small accounts that I seldom have the chance to go after the bigger and more profitable ones. So I'm going to use the long weekend to work on that, and I certainly won't have time left over for a baby."

He put a hand on her arm and deliberately focused every ounce of charm he could muster. "Help me out this weekend, Kady, and I'll get you all the new clients you can handle."

To his disappointment, the charm seemed to bounce off her. What was the woman made of, anyway? Armor?

"You? That I'd like to see."

"Then help," he said crisply. "Or if you'd rather play it the other way, listen to this. If you don't help, I'll make sure you never get any new clients." He held out both hands, as if to say he was sorry but he couldn't help the circumstances, that was just the way things were.

"Thanks for the oh, so generous offer, Devlin, but—" Without a hint of warning, she plopped the baby in his outstretched arms.

Sam started to shriek.

"It certainly *feels* like he's got a personal grudge," Devlin muttered. He was rapidly discovering that holding a greased pig would be a piece of cake compared to hanging onto an infant who definitely wanted to be elsewhere.

The baby stretched almost like a rubber doll, nearly flinging himself out of Devlin's arms in an effort to reach Kady.

Devlin watched as she bit her lip. He saw the shadow that flitted across her face. He noted the pain in her eyes as she watched the baby, and he wondered if she was remembering what it was like to be a child alone in an unfamiliar world—a disadvantaged child who'd spent nine years in an orphanage…all right, a group home. It didn't sound much different to him.

Sam was wailing in what sounded like agony.

"Please," Devlin heard himself say. The earnest note in his voice surprised him almost as much as it obviously did her. "Please, Kady. For Sam's sake."

She hesitated.

Devlin didn't breathe. After the longest moment in his life, she held out her arms, and Sam clambered eagerly into her embrace.

"The weekend, Devlin," she said firmly. "But that's all."

He nodded. "I'm sure I'll have it straightened out by then."

"You'd better, or you'll have to cope on your own the way a million other single parents do. And don't forget I'm only doing this because you so obviously don't have a prayer of managing by yourself, and this baby is too sweet to risk in your care. You'd probably feed him popcorn for dinner.''

''You mean I shouldn't?'' he said innocently. He patted the golden fuzz of curls on the child's head. Sam eyed him warily, his tiny fingers clutching Kady's jacket. He was obviously determined not to be dislodged again.

Maybe he does take after me, Devlin thought. *At least the kid knows a good thing when he sees it.*

Kady saw the light of satisfaction dawn in Devlin's eyes, and she had to exert all her willpower to keep from punching him. So he thought he'd solved his problem by handing it over to her, did he? Well, if there wasn't a baby at stake—a living, breathing, *feeling* baby—she'd walk out this minute and see how he managed.

Still, she couldn't exactly regret giving in, not when Sam's soft baby breath was tickling her neck. Not when his compact little body was nestled so trustingly against her. She stroked his back and felt him relax.

Devlin retrieved his popcorn from the microwave, slit the bag open to release the steam and offered it to Kady. She shook her head, and he took a handful.

''All right,'' he said, his tone businesslike. ''The first thing is to figure out who his mother is, so I'll—''

Kady interrupted. ''No. The first thing is to get the equipment you're going to need.''

''Like what?''

''A crib of some sort. He can't exactly sleep in your water bed, you know.''

''That's good,'' Devlin said. ''Especially since I don't have one.''

''You amaze me. And you'll need bottles and pajamas and baby wipes—and I think we're in urgent need of a fresh diaper.'' She sniffed and frowned. ''Wouldn't you think his mother would have included one extra, at least?''

If I was packing up my baby, she thought, *I'd make darned sure he had all the necessary equipment.* She'd send along his favorite stuffed toy, his teething ring, his best clothes—everything he might need to keep him safe and comfortable. But the only things this kid had come equipped with were a car seat and a blanket—as if his mother didn't much care.

The thought left Kady cold. She couldn't begin to imagine, much less understand, a woman who could turn her child over to a complete stranger.

Of course, Devlin wasn't exactly a stranger to Sam's mother, Kady admitted. But as far as the baby was concerned, he might as well have been dropped on the outermost ring of Saturn. How could anybody be so cruel?

The pressures that woman felt must be immense, far beyond Kady's comprehension. She couldn't imagine anything horrible enough to make her give away a baby she had borne, loved, nurtured, raised for the better part of a year—

''Maybe the taxi driver was so anxious to get rid of him that he forgot the luggage,'' Devlin said. ''Okay, you're in charge of equipment. Write a check on my account—or would you rather have my credit card?''

Kady stared at him.

''Well?''

''You needn't think I'm going to take care of it by myself, Devlin. Whose kid is this, anyway?''

''At the moment, I'd say that remains open to question.''

''Anybody with the intelligence of a dustpan can see the resemblance. Come on—if you're going to be ready to take full responsibility by Monday, you've got some learning to do.''

''What do you mean, Monday? You agreed to the

weekend, and with the holiday, this one's four days long.''

"I didn't mean—"

"Though I expect I'll have figured something out long before then. Since the Fourth of July isn't actually till Tuesday, all the social agencies will be open on Monday, won't they?''

Kady's heart jolted. "You wouldn't turn this baby over to the authorities, would you?''

"Why not? Isn't that what they're for? To take care of children who don't have regular homes?''

"This is certainly shaping up as an *irregular* one,'' Kady muttered. "But I wouldn't advise it—they'd have a lot of uncomfortable questions for you, like exactly why the baby ended up on *your* hands. And the story would probably get into the newspapers.''

"I'm not that newsworthy. The Cunninghams have always been a quiet sort of family—''

"Being a Cunningham has nothing to do with it. Haven't you considered the headline potential in the story of a baby abandoned on a man's doorstep?''

"Oh. I see what you mean.''

"And wouldn't that be a wonderful surprise for Iris when she gets home on Tuesday? Her grandson splashed over the front pages with the son he didn't know about....''

"All right, you've made your point. The social agencies are out.''

"So unless you can remember who Sam's mother might be and negotiate a deal to give him back, it looks to me as if you're stuck. You might as well learn how to shop for a baby's needs.''

She set Sam in his car seat once more. The child objected vociferously, reaching pleading arms up to Kady.

"Sorry, darling,'' she said firmly. "Safety first.''

"Do you suppose he's got a pin sticking him?" Devlin asked.

"Modern-day diapers don't have pins. Honestly, Devlin, don't you know anything about babies?"

"No," he said simply. "I'm the only child of an only child—so I don't even have a niece or a nephew, I'm afraid."

She looked at him for a long moment, then busied herself strapping the baby into his seat. "Sam," she said, "maybe I should warn you. You're in for one heck of an adventure here."

Devlin's car was a two-door sports model with an infinitesimal back seat, and it took both of them to maneuver Sam's baby chair into place and strap it down.

"I feel like a contortionist," Devlin said as he settled into the driver's seat.

"Get used to it," Kady murmured unsympathetically. "Or get a different car." She flipped open her appointment book, ripped out a page and started making a list.

Devlin started the car. "Where are we going?"

"To the nearest discount store. Or do you know where to find one? Obviously you don't shop at that sort of place often, but—"

"Funny. You're straight out of the comics."

"What a compliment," Kady said sweetly, "coming from someone who knows all about them!"

Sam was whimpering by the time they reached the store, and Kady briskly wheeled their cart to the baby department, chose a package of disposable diapers and ripped it open right in the aisle. "If anybody asks what happened to the package, tell them it was an emergency," she instructed Devlin. "I'll be back in a minute—unless you'd like to try your hand at a diaper change?"

Devlin shook his head and admitted, "I'm amazed you're volunteering."

"Sam's miserable, and there's no point in making him more so in order to give you a lesson. You'll have plenty of chances before the weekend's over." She thrust her list at him. "In the meantime, you can look for this stuff."

Once he was clean and dry, Sam actually smiled at her, and Kady's heart threatened to turn over. What a tiny, trusting, lovable baby he was. She could cheerfully throttle the woman who had so callously abandoned him.

She settled for blowing gently on his tummy as she straightened his shorts, and he chuckled—a low, rich sound that reminded her of Devlin—and clutched at a loose strand of her hair.

Devlin was at the end of the aisle full of baby goods, leaning against the cart and smiling at a brunette who was hanging onto his arm and talking fast. "I just had to come and tell you hello," she was saying as Kady came up. "It's been so long since I saw you. What have you been up to, anyway?" She spotted Kady, and her mouth dropped open. "Well, you have changed, haven't you, Devlin? I had no idea you'd consider dating a woman with children."

"He'd never think of it," Kady said cheerfully. "Have you got everything on your list, Devlin? Because I think your son's getting hungry, and—"

"*Your* son?" the brunette snapped.

"You certainly didn't think he was mine, did you?" Kady's eyes widened in mock astonishment. "He doesn't look a bit like me, you know."

The brunette muttered, "Lucky for him," and turned on her heel.

"Happy?" Devlin asked calmly. "Now that you've routed her—"

"I wouldn't call it a rout, exactly, but that's one of your acquaintances you don't need to track down and question. How many are left, do you suppose? Never mind—I don't think I want to know. Is there a reason you're just standing in front of the baby shampoo instead of putting some in the cart?"

"I was looking for a smaller package."

"It's less expensive in quantity."

"But there's enough in this bottle to shampoo Chicago. How much do you think we're going to need?"

"Oh, be a sport. Assuming you find Sam's mother and convince her to change her mind, you can send him back better equipped than he came."

Devlin put the shampoo in the cart.

Kady went on with a tinge of mischief, "She might be so grateful she'll let you have visitation. Just think, you could have Sam every other weekend and half of the summer—"

Devlin groaned.

Kady swallowed her smile. "It would be easier than having him all the time. I think we should look at a travel-size crib. That way you can set it up anywhere you want. You can even take it on an airplane, because when it's folded up, it's only the size of a golf bag."

Devlin seemed to have lost the power of speech.

"And we still need bottles and spoons and some clothes," Kady went on. "It's a wonder the kid hasn't needed a full change before this. And formula—"

She looked down the row of infant formula and bit her lip. When had the manufacturers started producing so many varieties? And why hadn't Sam's mother been decent enough to mention what brand she used, so at least the child would have the comfort of familiar food?

I hope Devlin finds that woman, Kady thought. *Because I'm going to have a few things to say to her, too.*

Sam went to sleep on the way home, and even when Kady picked him up from his car seat he didn't rouse fully but only snuggled against her with a baby snore.

Despite his unconscious state, however, he was fiercely clutching the stuffed giraffe he'd picked out in the toy department. Devlin had looked at her as if she was nuts when she'd held the baby up to make his choice, but it seemed to have been a good idea. At least now Sam had a cuddly friend.

"I hate to wake him," she said, standing in the middle of the kitchen with the baby in her arms.

"Then don't," Devlin said. He was making his second trip from the car, loaded down with their purchases. "I can't believe that a mere twenty pounds of kid needs half a ton of equipment."

Kady wasn't listening. "But he's got to be starved. He hasn't eaten since he got here." She sighed and flicked the baby's cheek with a gentle finger. "Come on, Sam. Rise and shine. It's dinnertime."

Sam yawned and snuggled closer. Kady sighed and balanced him in one arm while she struggled to fill a bottle with the other hand. Fully relaxed, he seemed to weigh about three times as much as normal.

Devlin was carrying in the last load of bags when she managed to rouse Sam enough to get the nipple in his mouth. He made a face, spit it out and howled.

"I told you not to wake him," Devlin said.

"If you want to take over, Cunningham, just keep up the running commentary."

"I didn't say a word," he assured her. "I'm a little worried about you, Kady. Do you often have delusions about hearing voices coming from nowhere?"

Kady tried the bottle again. Sam shoved it away and howled louder.

"Do you know what we forgot?" Devlin asked helpfully.

"You mean besides the other dozen brands of formula?"

"Something for *us* to eat. Do you like Chinese?

There's a place right around the corner called the Bamboo Orchid. I'll run over and get—'' Kady fixed him with a glare, and Devlin added smoothly, ''I'll call for delivery right now.''

''I wonder if he'd rather have regular milk,'' Kady mused. ''Maybe he's old enough to be off formula altogether. Or maybe, heaven help us, he's a breast-fed baby... No, the sort of heartless creature who dumped him here wouldn't have put herself to that much inconvenience.''

Devlin was already on the phone. It was obvious from the brisk way he recited his order that he'd done it a thousand times before. ''And send along a couple of glasses of milk, too,'' he added. ''Yes, plain ordinary milk.'' He paused. ''No, I got a sudden urge to try some in my bath, all right? Just send it.''

''Thanks,'' Kady said. ''For the milk, I mean.'' She gave up on the bottle and set Sam upright on her lap.

He stared at her with tear-drenched big brown eyes, stuck all four fingers of his right hand into his mouth and started to chew.

''I hope it doesn't take long,'' she fretted. ''He's got to be starving. Poor little guy, snatched away from everything familiar and set down among strangers, with a new routine, new food—''

''You make it sound sort of like military basic training,'' Devlin muttered.

''Isn't it? Wait a minute—didn't you say there was yogurt in the refrigerator? Maybe he'll take that.''

Sam adored yogurt. Kady was still spooning it into his mouth as fast as she could when the restaurant's busboy appeared at the back door with their order. Sam and the busboy eyed each other with evident interest while Devlin paid the bill, then the busboy left and Sam turned his attention to the contents of the fascinating waxed paper boxes. He was so intrigued he forgot to

swallow, and strawberry yogurt dribbled out of the corners of his mouth and down the front of his shirt.

"Here." Devlin started to hand her a cup of milk, but
Sam reached for it instead, and smiled at him.

"Well," Devlin said, "if that isn't a breakthrough,
I've never seen one."

Kady could understand why he sounded a bit stunned.
Sam had the most delightful smile she'd ever seen a
baby display. And by turning it on his father...

That's great, Kady thought. Now that Sam was dry
and fed, the two of them might actually start hitting it
off so well they wouldn't need her anymore.

And that, she told herself firmly, was just fine with
her, because she had more important things to do.

She snuggled Sam a little closer, and when Devlin
wasn't looking, she dropped a soft kiss on the baby's
curls.

The Chinese food was wonderful. Sam gnawed on a fortune cookie while Devlin and Kady polished off the best
Mandarin duck and Mongolian beef she'd ever tasted,
right down to the last scrap of steamed rice.

The coffee Devlin brewed after they'd finished eating
tasted better yet as far as Kady was concerned, though
Sam showed considerable interest in her cup and she
finally had to push it across the table to keep it out of
his reach.

"What kind of mother do you have, anyway," she
grumbled, "that you have a fondness for coffee?"

"Well, think about it," Devlin said reasonably. "Everything he's consumed tonight was cold."

Kady nibbled her fingernail. "You know, you show
promise of having some parental sense despite yourself."

"Heaven forbid." He gathered up the empty containers and carried them to the garbage bin, then refilled

Kady's cup and edged it slightly closer, so she could reach it but Sam couldn't. "Where do you want me to set up the crib?"

"Wherever Sam can't reach something he shouldn't get into."

"How about in the deserts of Arizona?"

Sam chortled and pounded the remains of his fortune cookie on the edge of the table, sending fragments cascading onto the floor.

Devlin stretched out a finger toward the baby's face. "So you think I'm pretty funny, little guy?"

Kady couldn't keep from laughing.

"And as for you, young woman," Devlin said. His finger flicked Sam's cheek and moved on to rest against Kady's face for an instant. Then his hand slid gently down the side of her throat and came to rest on the nape of her neck.

She was afraid to breathe, afraid to move. Slowly, he was leaning closer and closer yet. And he was watching her mouth, she realized, as if it was a succulent morsel of food he was planning to taste, just as soon as he'd fully savored the sight....

Kady couldn't help it. She instinctively licked her lower lip, and an instant later, Devlin's mouth brushed hers. The contact was light, but the sensation was like being hit by a flamethrower, as every muscle in her body quivered and then seemed to melt.

Sam said, "No!" and put his hand against Devlin's chin in a futile attempt to push him away. Then he dropped the rest of his cookie and hid his face against Kady's shoulder.

Cautiously, she sat back in her chair and shifted the baby's weight to a more comfortable position. "About that crib, Devlin." Her voice was unsteady. "Sam looks as if he'll need it pretty soon."

Slowly, Devlin withdrew his hand from the nape of

her neck. "We'll see if you're right about how easy it is to set up."

Even after he'd left the room, she was still tense. The kiss might have been light and fleeting, but the aftereffects were something like being hit by a truck. What was wrong with her, anyway, to allow that? And what had gotten into him? Was the man simply so used to having a woman around that anyone would do?

Sam wriggled, nuzzled and fussed a bit, and Kady cuddled him closer and started to sing, a low, soft melody that wasn't a lullaby but could have been. Slowly, he relaxed, and his eyes fluttered closed.

She didn't hear Devlin come back till he said, with a ripple of laughter in his voice, "Better watch where you put your hands, Sam—in a few years you'll be getting slapped for that."

She looked down. Sam had smeared the half-chewed remains of his fortune cookie on her tailored black blouse, directly over her left breast.

"It'll wash," she said.

Devlin pulled a chair out from the table. "Don't let me stop you from singing to him. You have a very pretty voice."

"Thanks. But he's asleep. Where did you put the crib?"

"Upstairs, in my bedroom. There isn't anywhere else."

She carried Sam up the two long flights, telling herself that the climb was the reason she was a bit breathless. She wasn't used to the weight of a sleeping child. Her discomfort had nothing to do with that tentative kiss. And it certainly wasn't because for the first time ever she was venturing into Devlin's private quarters, either.

At the top of the stairs she passed a half-open door that was obviously some kind of study and went past a black-tiled bathroom toward the front of the house.

Moonlight filtering through casual blinds on the front windows let her see that the bedroom was huge, occupying the entire width of the town house. A king-size bed took up a good part of the room, but there was still plenty of empty space, and Devlin had set the crib up in the middle of it. The furniture was nice, but not at all the sort she'd half-expected to see. There was no leopard skin bedspread, no mirrored canopy. Everything was simple, solid and comfortable-looking.

She put Sam down on his side. He half-woke and whimpered, and Kady patted his back and murmured a little song till he sighed and relaxed once more.

"Well," she said very softly. "Now that he's asleep, I'm going home to—"

Devlin's hand closed on her arm. "But you can't leave. You said you'd stay the weekend!"

"I did not. I said I'd help you out."

"What if he wakes up?"

"Pat him gently on the back and talk softly to him till he goes to sleep again." She eased past him and started down the stairs. "Anyway, I can't stay here, Devlin."

"Why on earth not? Judging by what happened a few minutes ago, you have the world's most efficient chaperon. So if you're worried about me trying to kiss you again—"

Kady willed herself not to change color. "Of course not. That has nothing to do with it. I simply want a shower, and I don't have any extra clothes—"

"I have a shower, and you may help yourself to anything in my closet. And I'm sure I've got an extra toothbrush—brand new, never out of the package."

"Why am I not surprised about that?" she muttered. "You probably buy them by the carton." She paused at the front door and patted back a fierce yawn. To tell the truth, she wasn't looking forward to driving across the city at this hour of the night. "I'll leave my computer, if you don't mind—I just don't feel like walking down to the kitchen after it. And I'll be here in the morning in plenty of time to show you how to give Sam his bath."

"Kady—" He was rubbing his chin as he came down the steps.

No doubt, Kady thought, he was planning his next strategy. She didn't intend to hang around and let him polish it up.

She opened the door and saw flashing lights on the street. Police? she wondered. Fire engines? The lights were yellow, though. It was just an auto club truck, probably helping someone with an overheated engine or a dead battery.

A banshee wail reverberated down the stairs.

"I told you so," Devlin said, with an air of triumph. "There he goes."

Kady wasn't listening. She was watching with horror as the yellow lights disappeared down the street with a car—its front wheels in the air—trailing behind.

It hadn't been an auto club truck helping a stranded motorist, but a wrecker clearing illegally parked cars from the limited-time spaces across the street.

And it was her car—the car she had parked this afternoon in a two-hour zone, and then completely forgotten—that was vanishing into the distance.

CHAPTER THREE

DEVLIN hadn't even reached the bottom of the stairs before Kady went out the door as if a swarm of killer bees was after her. She could protest all she wanted, he thought, but he knew better—she was running from that kiss. He wondered if it had been only his imagination that made him think he had, for just an instant, tasted willingness as sweet as honey on her lips.

Sam shrieked again.

Devlin banged the heel of his hand against his forehead and muttered, "Cunningham, you idiot—you had to go and mess up a good deal. The damned *baby's* got better sense than you do!"

Sam's wails escalated, and Devlin sighed and turned toward the stairs. "It looks like you and me, kid," he said. "Guess you'll just have to get used to it."

Sam was standing up in the travel crib when Devlin came in. The baby's face was bright red, his mouth was so wide open that he was almost unrecognizable, and as for the noise he was emitting...

Pat him on the back and talk to him, Kady had said. Yeah—a lot of good that was going to do!

Devlin leaned over the crib, and Sam shook his head violently.

"I see," Devlin said. "You're only civil to me when I have food, right?"

Sam screamed. Then, abruptly, he stopped screaming—and stopped breathing, as well.

Devlin snatched him out of the crib and ran for the stairs. Maybe if he did a record hundred-yard dash down the street, Kady would see him as she drove away and realize something was terribly wrong.

He took the stairs in three leaps and reached the bottom just as Kady opened the front door. Devlin had never seen any sight so beautiful in all his life. "Thank God," he whispered, and thrust the baby at her.

"My car's been towed, and you say thank God?"

"Sam's not breathing."

She held the infant at arm's length. "Yes, he is."

Devlin stared at the baby. Sam's face was tear-drenched and still flushed from his fit, but he was smiling at Kady.

"Well, he wasn't a minute ago," he said feebly. "He was screaming his lungs out, and then all of a sudden he stopped making noise and I thought he'd burst something."

"He was having a temper tantrum. You probably startled him out of it when you picked him up—poor little guy."

"Poor little guy? Him?" Devlin said, unbelievingly. "What about *me*? He scares me to death, and you sympathize with him?"

"Well, you have to admit Sam's had a rough day. If the only way you could make your point was to scream, I bet you'd be a champion." She paused. "Devlin, what am I going to do about my car?"

He hardly heard her. He was watching the tremulous quivering of her full lower lip and telling himself firmly that under no circumstances should he attempt to stop that quaver with either his fingertip or his mouth. If he did, she'd run again, and then he and Sam would be seriously up a creek.

Still, it took real effort to push the thought away. That

trembling lip was a royal temptation. "We'll deal with it tomorrow."

She sighed. "I suppose you're right—there's no point in chasing the wrecker."

"You mean they took it just now? Is that why you ran out?"

"Of course." The baby had snuggled close to her, and she was shifting her weight slowly from one foot to the other. "Surely you didn't think I was dodging you?"

That's one in the eye, Cunningham, he told himself. "Why are you doing that?"

"What? Rocking him? I don't know—it seems to be a female thing. Hand almost any woman a baby and she automatically starts. Speaking of which, you wouldn't happen to have a rocking chair, would you?"

Devlin shook his head. "I've never had a need for anything of the sort."

"Maybe you should consider buying one. It would make things easier on you."

"A straitjacket might work even better," Devlin muttered.

"Do you mean Sam's size, or yours?" Kady didn't wait for an answer. "Would you bring the diapers upstairs in case he needs a change? Then I'll get him settled again."

And she probably could, Devlin thought. Inexplicably, the thought annoyed him. Why should the kid show such a decided preference for her, anyway? Maybe it was because she was so incredibly feminine, despite that tailored suit.

There were worse reasons, he decided. Sam had pretty good taste, all things considered.

Kady started up the stairs, crooning to Sam.

"Make yourself comfortable," Devlin called after her. He couldn't quite keep the note of irony out of his voice.

Kady obviously heard it, for she leaned over the banister and said, "I'll certainly have to try."

He grinned. Suddenly, he felt a whole lot better.

Sam had gotten just enough rest to take the edge off his weariness. And, Kady soon realized, he'd also figured out that going to sleep meant his chosen caretaker might disappear again. After all, she'd done so before.

"Nothing slow about the way your mind works, is there, Sam?" Kady murmured as she put him down on the king-size bed to change him. "That was very bad judgment on my part, letting you learn that lesson. How can I convince you I'll still be here whenever you wake up?"

But Sam was not to be convinced. He fought with every weapon at his command to keep his eyes open. He fussed, he struggled, he wriggled—and every time Kady thought he'd dozed off despite himself and tried to put him down in the crib, he startled awake and started to yell. Finally she gave up and settled herself on Devlin's bed, propped against the tall carved headboard with the baby cradled in her arms.

At this rate, it was going to be a very long night.

Devlin lounged in the door of his bedroom and watched. "You look pretty uncomfortable in that skirt, Kady."

"Well, give the man a medal," she muttered crossly.

"Have you tried patting him on the back and talking to him?" he asked, with an air of helpfulness. "I seem to remember an expert telling me that's the best way to—"

Kady picked up a comic book from the bedside table and flung it at him.

"Hey, that's a volume one, number one Crime Stompers," he protested. "A first edition, to nonbelievers like you. And it used to be in mint condition."

"So what? You probably have a dozen of them."

"More like a hundred, actually. But—"

"So if you don't want me to toss it at you again, go away. Every time you make a noise Sam rouses up."

Devlin smoothed the cover of the comic book. He looked almost wounded, but Kady didn't think for a minute he really felt that way. "I'll be in my study if you need me." His soft, minor-key whistle faded away down the hall.

It would serve him right if I handed the kid over and called a cab, Kady told herself. Instead, she cradled Sam even closer and whispered, "I'm not going anywhere, baby. I'm right here."

Sam grunted a protest, but he closed his eyes.

Kady leaned against a stack of pillows and tried to relax. Despite the strain of a long day, she was too keyed up to rest. She was dead tired, but not at all sleepy. It must have been the coffee, she thought, that had speeded up her heart rate and sent her thoughts into orbit.

At least, she hoped it was the coffee, and not Devlin's kiss—but whenever she closed her eyes, she found herself remembering the way Devlin's mouth had felt against hers, scorching and yet soothing all at the same time. It had been the most unusual kiss she'd ever experienced, she'd grant him that distinction. Just thinking about it made her muscles feel like a sack of chocolate drops on a warm afternoon—not quite liquid, but certainly not in their normal state, either....

She'd shed her jacket, but her skirt had ridden up and was twisted, and her blouse was binding across her shoulders till Kady couldn't stand it anymore. She studied the baby's face for a full minute, and when he didn't make a noise she cautiously eased him onto the bedspread, tucked his blanket around him and laid a pillow carefully on each side. He'd be safe that way for a few minutes while she made herself more comfortable.

The question was how to do that. *Help yourself to anything in my closet,* Devlin had said. She wondered if he maintained a wardrobe for his women friends.

But there was no sign of feminine clothes. Kady peeked gingerly through the drawers built into the bottom of the closet. There was also, she noted, no sign of pajamas. Well, that was no surprise, surely?

Sam made a gurgling sound and twisted onto his side, and Kady froze. He subsided into silence once more, but, knowing the peace might not last long, she seized an oversize T-shirt and a pair of boxer shorts from a drawer and told herself the combination wasn't so very different from the pajamas she wore at home.

Though of course she wasn't in the habit of wearing royal blue satin boxer shorts. She wondered which of the women in his life was responsible for that particularly exotic piece of apparel. Surely Devlin wasn't egotistical enough to have bought the shorts himself. Had they been the gift of the brunette they'd run into at the discount store, perhaps? She'd struck Kady as the royal blue satin type.

The combination was startlingly comfortable. She settled on the bed again and curled up on her side. As if attracted by her warmth, Sam wriggled closer.

The room wasn't as huge as she'd thought originally, even though it occupied the whole width of the town house. Its apparent size was partly because of the lack of furniture, she realized. Except for the bed, a pair of night tables and an entertainment center that filled the entire opposite wall, there was nothing in the room except Sam's empty crib.

Idly, with nothing else to occupy her mind, Kady catalogued the entertainment center. It contained a big-screen television with all the associated video equipment anyone could want, a half dozen shelves of books and a stereo setup that looked like the last word in sound quality. The closed cabinets across the bottom of the entire wall must hide Devlin's CDs and videos. Obviously he spent a lot of time here—but since he didn't have a living room to entertain in...

Of course *that*, she thought, was probably by design!

Devlin had finally dozed off beside his desk in the only marginally comfortable chair in the town house, and he woke with a stiff neck to a silence so blessedly complete that for a moment he tried to convince himself Sam had been only a particularly vivid nightmare. Then he saw the list of names on his desk blotter, and the silence began to feel threatening instead of comforting. Was it too quiet?

Suspicion nibbled at the corners of his mind. What did he really know about Kady Bishop, anyway? He had only her word for the story of the taxi driver. She could even have composed the note herself. He'd never seen enough of her handwriting to be any judge. She'd talked him out of calling the authorities. And Sam was so incredibly at ease with her—as if she wasn't really a stranger.

What if the whole thing was a setup? Some kind of scam?

He tiptoed down the hall to his bedroom.

Kady was sound asleep, curled on her side with her back to the door, her hair a tangled mass of blue-black against the white pillow and her cheek snuggled against Sam's stuffed giraffe. Devlin watched her for a full minute, and the suspicion inside him relaxed a little. What on earth would she have to gain from a scheme like this?

He'd never seen her hair down before, and he hadn't expected it to be so long and silky. What a waste it was to keep it pinned up in a knot!

And though he'd had a good idea from the first time he'd met her how long and shapely her legs were, he could never have imagined how stunning she'd look wearing his blue satin boxers. The shorts had been a gag gift one Christmas, laughed over and then tucked out of sight. It had never occurred to Devlin that they could be so very sexy. And the oversize T-shirt from his alma mater was just as attractive. The knit draped around her, doing nothing to hide the softly sculptured curves of her body.

In fact, everything about her invited him to touch. His fingertips tingled at the idea, and he found himself easing closer to the bed.

She sighed and turned slightly, and the T-shirt re-draped itself, molding her breasts.

In the back of his mind doubt quivered to life once more. Still, he thought, if she'd had any idea of entrapping him, surely she'd have put her natural resources to better use long before now.

Not that it mattered to him whether she was really the prim and proper accountant she'd seemed for the past six months, or the sultry temptress who was occupying his bed right now. His life was complex enough at the moment without adding *either* version of Kady Bishop to his list of complications.

Nevertheless, he'd make darned sure she stayed where he could keep an eye on her.

Oh, that's humorous, Cunningham, he told himself. The problem at the moment was going to be taking his eyes *off* her.

Kady's hand rested lightly across the baby's stomach, as if to assure her that he was safe. Sam was sprawled flat on his back, taking up an immense amount of the bed for such a little guy. No wonder Kady had insisted on buying warm pajamas for him despite the season, for Sam had kicked his blanket aside.

Devlin stood looking at the pair for a long while. Then he covered them both with the bedspread and went to his study, to sit staring once more at the list he'd made last night.

Somewhere on that list was Sam's mother. She had to be.

And it was becoming increasingly important to Devlin that he find her just as soon as possible.

A tiny, confused, mournful cry woke Kady. She came to full awareness in little more than a split second, sitting bolt upright in the bed.

Sam was sitting up, too, his brow furrowed and eyes wide with fright. He climbed into Kady's arms and clung, and her heart melted. "Poor little fellow," she whispered. "It's quite enough of a shock for me, waking up in Devlin's bed. I can't imagine how you must feel about it!"

She glanced at the crumpled wreck of her linen suit, hanging where she'd left it draped over the rail of Sam's crib. It had been foolish to hope that the wrinkles would hang out overnight, and now there didn't seem to be any alternative to going around looking as if she'd slept in her clothes.

Of course, she thought idly, if anyone was ever to discover that she'd spent the night in Devlin Cunningham's bed, looking crumpled might be better for her reputation than if she appeared neat and pressed.

She glanced into the bathroom on the off-chance that Devlin might own a travel iron and raised an eyebrow at the two-person black marble whirlpool tub that occupied an elevated platform in the center of the room. She certainly couldn't give Sam a bath in that. It would probably take half the day to fill. Besides, she thought, it would be like dunking the kid in a swimming pool. He'd no doubt be terrified.

Sam started to fuss.

"Are you hungry?" Kady asked.

He merely looked at her.

"A young man of very few words, I perceive," she murmured, and gave up the idea of getting dressed till after she'd dealt with his breakfast. She found a dark red brocade affair hanging at the back of Devlin's closet. Though she supposed it had been meant as a sort of smoking jacket, on her it was long enough to double as a robe. She put it on and picked Sam up.

She could hear the rise and fall of Devlin's voice from his study, and she paused before going into the hall. Surely he wouldn't have anyone with him, would he? She could discern only one voice, however. She concluded he must be on the telephone, getting an early start on his research project.

Sam, impatient with their lack of progress, let out a furious yell. A moment later, she heard Devlin say, "What do you mean, where did the baby come from? I didn't pick him up on the rack at the corner drugstore, that's for sure."

She wanted to applaud the woman on the other end of the line, whoever she was. Any man who needed even a moment to think about the question Devlin was struggling with deserved all the discomfort he got!

Sam eyed the rice cereal she'd bought with disdain, but ultimately—after Kady mixed the rest of the strawberry yogurt into the dish—he condescended to eat it. By the time his hunger was soothed, he had cereal stuck to his ears, caked in his hair and solidly layered down the front of his pajamas. He even had cereal in his eyelashes—and his fingers, Kady saw, might as well have been glued together.

With a sigh, she filled the kitchen sink with warm water, plopped him in and handed him the yogurt container to play with. He promptly poured the first cup of water down the sleeve of her robe and giggled when she gasped as the deluge hit her.

Kady slid out of the dripping red wrap and draped it over the nearest chair to dry. The expensive brocade would probably never be the same—but Devlin had only himself to blame. Whether he would see it that way, however, might be a different question.

She washed Sam's hair, over his protests, and soaped and rinsed the wriggly little body. As she started to lift him out, however, he said, "No!" and held desperately—if futilely—to the slick edge of the sink.

"Do you want to play in the water now that the uncomfortable part's done?" Kady asked.

Sam didn't answer. He sat down with a splash, picked up the yogurt cup and dipped it into the water.

"Oh, I get it. You only bother to talk when you're strongly opposed to the question at hand—so silence must mean you're agreeable. Right?"

Sam grinned approvingly and dumped water over his chest.

"Have a good time," Kady said. She yawned and wished that there was a more comfortable chair in the kitchen—or at least something to do. She couldn't move more than two steps from the sink, for the slick little fish was quite able to fling himself out of his bath and onto the floor before she could dash back and grab him. But she could foresee quite a period of boredom before he got tired of playing or the water cooled enough to force him out.

She stretched her foot toward the chair where she'd dumped her computer case the night before and pulled it toward her. She couldn't risk the computer getting wet, of course, but hadn't she stuck a book in a side pocket?

Sam played and babbled at her. Kady kept one eye on him to guard against splashes and the other on her book.

The division in her attention was probably why she didn't hear the click of a key in the kitchen door. The first warning Kady had was a stream of sunshine pouring in as the door opened, then a shadow falling across her. She whirled around and stared at the intruder.

Hal's mouth was hanging open most unattractively, and he was almost as bug-eyed as the caricatured villains in the comic books Devlin collected.

Sam grinned and banged his cup down in the water, sending a small tidal wave over Kady's T-shirt and her book.

Hal recovered first. "Well," he said. "I guess when you told me you had plans for the weekend, you really meant it."

Kady wanted to groan. Being caught standing in Devlin's kitchen, soaked to the skin, garbed in his underwear... Could things possibly get worse?

"Your kid?" Hal asked, waving a hand at Sam.

"Don't be silly."

"Then where'd he—she—come from?"

Devlin answered from the hallway. He was lounging against the door frame, barefoot and wearing jeans and a half-buttoned shirt. "The bank was giving away awards for every new customer. So I asked for a blond babe—but as you can see, somebody mixed up the order."

Hal's eyes had grown even wider at Devlin's appearance. "Whatever you say. Don't let me interrupt you, guys, I'm just passing through. I left my ID card in my desk yesterday, but I'll need it for the party tonight."

He breezed across the hall and up the stairs.

"Must be some party," Devlin said.

"You don't want to know." Kady mopped water off her arms, then lifted a protesting Sam out of the sink and wrapped him in a towel.

Hal was back inside of a minute. He flashed a wink at Kady and a thumbs-up sign to Devlin and said, "I don't suppose you want me to tell anyone?"

As if he could keep a secret, Kady thought, but before she could say anything Hal was gone. If it hadn't been for Sam's tender ears, she would have sworn.

Of course, she thought irritably, if it wasn't for Sam she wouldn't be in the midst of this mess in the first place. No, that wasn't fair—it was hardly the baby's fault. If it wasn't for *Devlin*, she'd have been peacefully at home writing letters to prospective customers.

"Is this yours?" he said. "Or is Sam such a prodigy he was reading in the tub?"

Kady frowned. "What?"

Devlin held up her book. Drips of water were rolling down the glossy cover. The embracing couple pictured there looked as if they'd gone for an unexpected swim.

"Oh. Give it back, please."

"I'll dry it off for you." He tore a long strip off a roll of paper towels beside the sink and began blotting.

With her hands full of damp, squirming child, Kady could hardly protest. She sat down on the floor, stood Sam between her knees and started to pat his skin dry.

"Not the kind of thing I expected you to be reading," Devlin observed.

Kady's voice was tart. "Just because I'm good at numbers doesn't mean I find it relaxing to read algebraic equations."

"Really? I'd think math would put me to sleep faster than anything else."

Sam wriggled free, plopped onto his hands and knees and took off in a mad scramble toward the door.

Kady lunged after him. Her hand slipped in the water he'd splashed out of the sink and she slid sideways, hitting the row of cabinets with a bang.

Fascinated by the noise, Sam paused and looked over his shoulder.

Devlin was beside her almost before she'd stopped sliding. "Kady—are you all right?"

"Fine, except for my pride. You'd better catch the baby before he gets to the stairs."

He crossed the room and scooped up Sam, ignoring the baby's protests. "How'd he manage to splash water clear over here?"

Kady looked at the puddle by Devlin's feet, then at Sam. Like all babies his age, when he wasn't wearing a diaper, he seemed to be all head and tummy.

"That's not water," she said glumly.

Just as she spoke, Devlin held the baby at arm's length. But he was too late. A dark, wet stain was spreading down the side of his jeans from his hip, where Sam had been resting an instant before.

Kady couldn't decide which was funnier, the stunned look on Devlin's face or the blissful relief on Sam's. She rolled over on her back and tried desperately to choke down her laughter.

Devlin, still holding Sam away from him, glared. Sam's face turned solemn.

Kady was laughing so hard tears were flowing down her cheeks. "What a good boy you are," she managed to gasp, "to finish the job for Daddy!"

Devlin set Sam down. The baby took two steps toward Kady, then his knees quivered and he sat down hard on the kitchen floor.

She sat up. "Did you see that? He walked!"

Devlin was brushing futilely at his jeans. "Wonderful. The next trick I'm going to teach him is to hitchhike. At this rate it's a skill he's going to need very soon."

"Oh, Devlin, be a sport. He actually walked!"

He paused and looked at the baby. "Hey," he said slowly. "He did, didn't he?"

She hugged Sam close. "What a big boy you are!"

The child stared at her, grinned, then reached up a tiny index finger and scooped a stray tear off her cheek.

Kady thought her heart would burst. What an incredible child this was! She smiled mistily at Devlin.

He wasn't looking at Sam. He was staring at her, and there was an expression in his dark brown eyes she didn't understand. She only knew it made her insides quiver—but whether it was fear or something else she was feeling, Kady couldn't begin to guess.

Steam from Kady's shower—a fast one, taken while Sam waited impatiently just outside the stall, pushing the curtain aside now and then to be sure she was still there—relaxed the wrinkles in her skirt enough to make it wearable. A pin-striped oxford-cloth shirt from Devlin's closet completed her ensemble. With the hem folded up in back and the tails knotted together at her waist, it almost looked as if it fit.

He was on the phone again when she went into his study. Sam waved his arms as if reaching for the telephone and babbled a string of nonsense, and Devlin grimaced.

He's waiting for the inevitable question, Kady thought, and leaned against the doorjamb to enjoy his discomfort.

"Yes, it's a baby." He sounded exasperated. "He was the dessert special at the restaurant last night, that's how I got him. Hey, it was nice to talk to you. Give my best to Jake, all right?" He put the phone down.

"Who's Jake?" Kady asked idly.

"Her husband. Nice guy."

Kady's jaw dropped. "A *married* one? And you like—" Her voice failed.

"Now she is." He drew a line through a name and slid the sheet of paper into the top drawer of his desk. "She wasn't when I was dating her."

"Oh. Well, that's a relief." Kady hadn't gotten a good enough look at the list to read the names, but she'd had no difficulty spotting how long it was. She told herself that the sinking feeling inside her was nothing more than irritation at the confirmation of what an irresponsible playboy Devlin was. "How foolish of me to think you might keep a little black book of the women you've dated, when the Chicago telephone directory serves the same purpose."

"Quite correct," Devlin said coolly. "It's far more efficient to just check off the names than have to write them all out again. Except for the ones with unlisted phones, of course—they're such a nuisance to keep track of."

Kady murmured, "There's no need to be sarcastic. *I'm* not the one who created that list—or the need for it."

Having the last word didn't create the sense of victory she'd expected, however. Though she supposed that was easy enough to explain. She was disillusioned, that was all, disappointed that a man as smart as Devlin Cunningham could be shortsighted enough to get himself into a mess like this.

CHAPTER FOUR

THE impound garage where Kady's car had been taken was in the next suburb, and the motion of Devlin's sports car as they drove across town lulled Sam to sleep within minutes.

At a stoplight, Devlin tipped the rearview mirror so he could see the baby's face. "We should have thought of taking him for a drive last night."

"Oh, I don't know if that would have done any good," Kady murmured. "I think this just means he's more like you than you care to admit. He even has his days and nights mixed up, just like—"

"I do not," Devlin said.

"Oh, I beg your pardon! The fact that you're never to be found before noon, and then you generally show up with a full day's growth of beard—"

"That's the key word, you know. A *day's* growth—not a night's."

Kady waved a hand. "Semantics," she announced. "I meant twenty-four hours' worth. The point is—"

"We're at the impound lot," Devlin interrupted. "Do you want to get your car back, or not?"

"You just don't like to lose an argument, do you, Devlin?" Humming, she slid out of the car and lifted Sam from his seat.

The baby didn't stir all through the wait, even when Kady shifted him into Devlin's arms because her own were growing numb.

"Cute baby," observed the woman in the office, while Kady was filling out the paperwork. "He looks a lot like his daddy."

"I certainly think so," Kady said sweetly. "Behaves like him, too."

Devlin gave her a sidelong look, moved Sam to his other shoulder and pulled out his wallet. "How much?" The woman told him, and he handed over a wad of cash that made Kady's throat go dry.

As soon as they were outside the building she said, "I'll pay you back."

"Don't worry about it. If it wasn't for Sam, the car wouldn't have been parked overtime in the first place."

"That's very thoughtful of you. But—"

Devlin finished airily, "So I'll just take it out of his allowance."

Kady decided not to push the subject. If Devlin agreed to let her repay him, she'd have to face the embarrassment of confessing that she couldn't do so at the moment unless he'd take her credit card. She'd had no idea how expensive towing and storage fees and fines were. And he had a point about where the responsibility lay— though it wasn't Sam's fault, of course, but his own.

"Want me to take him now?" she asked.

"Aren't you going to get your car?"

"Oh—I'd forgotten." She bit her lip. "What if he wakes up and I'm not there?"

"I'll drive faster," Devlin said dryly, "and put him back to sleep. I'll follow you, since I don't know where you live. We can drop off your car and go back to—"

"But I'll need it."

"No, you won't. And since parking is even tighter in my neighborhood on weekends when all the yuppie stockbrokers are at home, your car would probably just get towed again—and then where would you be?"

The argument was unanswerable, so Kady meekly

turned toward the corner of the lot where the woman had said her car was stored.

"I don't believe it," Devlin said as she walked away.

Kady spun around to face him, eyebrows lifted in inquiry.

"For a whole ten seconds now," he mused, "both you and Sam have been perfectly quiet. Maybe there are miracles, after all!"

Kady stuck her tongue out at him and started down the long row of cars.

A few minutes later she parked her car in its regular spot not far from her apartment and walked up to Devlin's window as he pulled in right behind her. "I've been thinking," she announced. "Since you want a rocking chair—"

"Are you sure of that?"

"Well, if you'd rather drive around all night, it's perfectly fine with me."

"I didn't say I wouldn't buy a rocking chair, just that I don't particularly want one."

"You're terrific at splitting hairs, Cunningham—has anyone ever told you that? Tyler-Royale's having a furniture sale at the Oak Park store, and if we went out there we could get Sam some more clothes, too. And speaking of clothes, I need to change." She let a hand drift down over her skirt. "Just wait here, I'll be right back."

Devlin frowned. "This wouldn't be a ploy to disappear and leave me holding the baby, would it?"

"Of course not. I promised you the weekend, and I'll keep my word."

Devlin grunted. "You know, when you start sounding virtuous I get worried."

"Besides, you're in a no-parking zone and if you leave the car, you might come back to find it's been towed."

"Foolish me," Devlin said wryly. "I ought to be ashamed of myself for being suspicious, when all the time you had my best interests at heart. Get in, Kady. If we're going to Tyler-Royale anyway, I'll just buy you something to wear."

"Why? I've got a perfectly good wardrobe in my apartment."

"Because whatever you say, I'm no more anxious to let you out of my sight than Sam is—and the last thing I want to do is climb into the back of the car and get him out of that baby seat an extra time so we can follow you."

Kady hesitated.

"Please, Kady?"

She gave in and settled herself in the passenger seat. "You've got more money than is good for you, you know."

"That's good news. You've been acting as if I'm going to run out before the end of next year."

"Keep on filling every scrap of space with comic books, and you will."

"Ah, but they'll be worth a lot more in the long run."

"Only if someone wants to buy them. It's not the amount of money you've got that matters so much anyway. I was speaking in relative terms. You've always had cash to fall back on, and it makes you act like an autocrat."

"All right, that does it. Wear rags, and see if I care."

"This suit isn't a rag." Kady tried to smooth the skirt, but the steam treatment had been only a temporary fix. In fact, now the wrinkles looked permanent. She sighed. "At least, it wasn't when I put it on yesterday—so I guess you're right, you owe me a suit."

"No, I don't. Sam does. At the rate he's incurring debts, the kid will be lucky if he has any of his allowance left by the time he's eighteen."

"See? I told you he was just like you," Kady murmured.

The Tyler-Royale store anchored one end of an enormous suburban mall. The store itself was huge. The women's clothing department filled an entire floor.

Kady had half-expected Devlin to wander off while she looked, but perhaps she'd underestimated his fear. Sam was still snoring in his arms, and Devlin seemed quite content to stick like glue to Kady's side as long as he was holding the baby.

She settled on two lightweight shorts sets, one in Chinese blue and the other in fuchsia. She was just coming back from the fitting room—half surprised that Devlin hadn't been waiting just outside the door—when she spotted a flowing jersey skirt on the clearance rack. It was no surprise to see it there, for it was an odd combination of pine green and purple. Few women could wear those colors, but Kady had learned they looked like dynamite on her. And the skirt *was* on the sales rack. Surely she could find some sort of jacket to coordinate with it.

She picked up the skirt just as a feminine voice in the next aisle called, "Devlin Cunningham! I haven't seen you in—"

Unable to stay away, Kady turned the corner to see the show. This one was a redhead. The man certainly liked variety, didn't he? Of course Shelle Emerson was a redhead, too—though this woman's hair was auburn, a couple of shades darker than Shelle's.

The woman's voice trailed off into silence as Devlin turned to face her, bringing her almost nose to nose with Sam. "Where'd you get a baby, Devlin?"

Kady had to bite her lip to keep from laughing at the sudden change from cultured tones to strident shock in the woman's voice. She couldn't have sounded more stunned if he'd been carrying a boa constrictor.

Devlin said, absolutely straight-faced, "He was delivered in a taxi. Kady! Are you done yet? My arms are getting tired."

She took Sam from him. The child blinked sleepily a couple of times and settled against her shoulder like a rag doll.

"Delivered in a taxi?" the redhead said faintly. She stared at Kady and said, with half-concealed spite, "Oh, my poor dear—was it dreadfully painful for you? It must have been horribly embarrassing to give birth in such a public place."

"Not at all," Kady said cheerfully.

The redhead's gaze wandered over Kady's rumpled clothes. "Of course, now I see that it probably wouldn't bother you at all."

"Because he isn't my baby," Kady went on, "just Devlin's."

The woman looked a little doubtful, so Kady added brightly, "We have that fact on the best of authority."

"Kady!"

She breezed straight on as if she hadn't heard the note of warning in Devlin's voice. "The taxi driver told us."

The redhead tossed her hair in a gesture worthy of Shelle Emerson at her best, but she didn't add another jab, just retreated into the elite salon where designer fashions were displayed.

Devlin glared at Kady.

She refused to be cowed. She stood up a little straighter and took careful note of the way he was standing, with his hands resting lightly on his hips. They were very nice hands, she thought, the fingers long and slender and sensitive. And very nice hips, too, under his snug-fitting jeans—narrow and perfectly proportioned. But of course there was no point in dwelling on facts like that. "Is she on your list?" Kady asked pleasantly.

Devlin's voice wasn't much more than a growl. "Is it any of your business?"

"Of course not. I was just thinking, though, that it would help me keep better track if I had a scorecard. Had you forgotten that you said you'd call Shelle?"

"What reminded you of her?"

Kady shrugged. "It was a leap in logic. That woman's hair color is no more real than Shelle's is. At any rate, you did say that you'd—"

"How would you know that Shelle dyes her hair?"

Kady blinked innocently. "You mean it *does* rub off on the pillowcases? I've often wondered, but—"

"I have no idea whether it does or not," Devlin growled. "I was just asking why you were so certain."

"Believe me, women know these things. Anyway, you said you'd call her this weekend—"

"No, I didn't. I said I'd call her sometime."

Kady frowned. "Well, maybe you're right. But if you've decided to take her to the picnic after all, you'd better give her some notice."

He groaned. "I'd forgotten the damned picnic. Can't we just tell the staff we came down with bubonic plague or something?"

"Of course we can't. I merely brought it up because I think you should buy a stroller as well as a rocking chair. Then if Sam wants to sleep all day tomorrow, you won't have to carry him."

"Don't you mean *we*?"

"You and Shelle?" Kady asked brightly.

Devlin shook his head.

She shrugged. "It was worth a try."

Disturbed by her movement, Sam raised his head and said very faintly, "Da-da."

"Well, would you listen to that," Devlin said. He sounded as if he'd been hit hard in the solar plexus.

Kady told herself she should be pleased, not half-annoyed. If he and Sam struck a peace treaty, she could go home. On the other hand, the tinge of pride in Devlin's voice grated on her. The man ought to be ashamed of himself for having a year-old son who was only now beginning to learn who he was, not proud of a half-conscious and probably meaningless phrase.

Her voice was sharp. "You don't seriously think he was asking for you, do you?"

"He distinctly said *daddy*. Surely you aren't going to try to convince me he was talking about you?"

"He did not say anything of the kind," Kady argued. "He made a babbling noise. It's one of the first sounds all babies make, and it has nothing to do with calling for their fathers."

"Kady," Devlin said calmly.

"How do you think the word *father* got corrupted into *daddy*, anyway? It makes no linguistic sense, but some egotistical father assumed that the first recognizable sound the kid made must refer to him, so he christened himself Daddy and the world's been stuck with the idea ever since. Men can be incredibly—"

"Kady, do you want a rocking chair or not?"

"At least *mama* bears a resemblance to the word it replaces. By the way, do you always change the subject when you're on the wrong end of an argument, Devlin?"

"Only when I'm dealing with you, since it seems to be the one way that works. Of course, if you'd rather, I could try out some alternatives, just to see what happens. For instance, whenever you have the bad taste to disagree with me, I could just kiss you until you change your mind."

The easy tone of his voice irritated Kady beyond words. The man really thought he was irresistible, didn't he? As if a simple kiss from him could make a woman forget her convictions, her beliefs, her standards...

On the other hand, she asked herself, was there such

a thing as a simple kiss if Devlin Cunningham was involved?

She couldn't help remembering the effect of that brush of his lips against hers last night. Brief and fleeting though the caress had been, the mere recollection of it still had the power to make her muscles quiver as if she was being jolted by an electrical current.

And that particular caress had been about as uncomplicated as a kiss could ever be. It had been over almost before it started, because of Sam's objections.

And yet, she wondered if it was fair to say it was over even now, so long as every time she thought about it the contact seemed to sizzle through her body once more.

"Maybe I should give you a demonstration," Devlin said.

She took an involuntary step back. "Why?"

"Because you look skeptical."

That, Kady thought, was exactly the problem. She wanted to believe he couldn't possibly exert that sort of power over her—but she wasn't so sure she could convince herself she was immune.

Oh, that was really cute, Cunningham, Devlin told himself. *What a positively stupid thing to threaten.* He must sound like a teenager who thought he was some kind of stud.

Just because every time he looked at Kady Bishop he found himself thinking she had the most kissable mouth in greater Chicago was no reason to pull that sort of Neanderthal stunt. It wasn't likely that a mere kiss could make the opinionated Miss Bishop change her mind, anyway.

No, it would take more than a kiss. Probably a great deal more—and the very idea of tackling that challenge made his mouth water.

He dropped back a couple of steps. The aisles really

were too narrow to let them walk side by side and still leave room for people coming in the opposite direction—but that fact also made a good excuse to follow her, so he could watch the kick of her skirt as she walked.

He wondered if Kady had any idea that the slight sway of her hips was far more feminine, more sensual, more inviting, than the exaggerated swagger so many women affected.

How had he ever let himself believe Kady looked so prim and proper because she really was that way? How had he missed the fire smoldering inside her?

He wondered just how difficult it would be to fan those lingering coals into full flame, to melt her resistance and reshape her desires in the heat of her own passion. The challenge might well provide the most fun he'd had in years.

Though of course, he'd be far better off if he skipped the experiment and instead reminded himself, every time he noticed that perfectly shaped mouth, of the sharp-edged tongue that was just as much a part of her....

The furniture department was on the second floor, and Devlin entertained himself on the slow ascent of the escalator by remembering the long slim lines of her legs, the soft curve of her hip, the intriguing swell of her breast, as he'd seen them just this morning while she slept.

After all, he told himself, it was safe enough to imagine what it would be like to take Kady Bishop to bed, since he had no intention of acting on the thought.

At the top of the escalator she paused to get her bearings, and as she turned toward the furniture department her hair, loose around her shoulders, brushed Devlin's arm. The satin caress and the soft scent of shampoo set his heart pounding, and he had to physically restrain himself from reaching out for a handful of the warm, silky, aromatic blue-black mass. But it wouldn't do to rush her....

Rush her? He reminded himself that he didn't plan to do anything at all. But if he were to set out to seduce her, he knew how he'd start his campaign—with simple touch. Soft, easy, almost accidental, until she gentled enough to welcome more. Then he'd stroke the contours of her face, the nape of her neck, the velvet underside of her arm above her elbow. Her skin would be as soft as Sam's. Devlin didn't understand why he was so certain, but he knew it, and his fingertips ached with the desire to explore every inch of that loveliness. Especially all the secret corners...

Kady sat down in a rocking chair and bounced out of it almost in the same movement, shaking her head. "The arms are at the wrong angle," she said. "You'd have pains in your shoulders in twenty minutes if you tried to rock Sam in that chair."

"How nice of you to be concerned for me."

"Oh, I'd feel terribly responsible if you couldn't play tennis any more because I chose the wrong chair."

She was good, he had to admit. There was only the barest hint of irony in her voice, and her eyes were wide and innocent. He hadn't noticed before that they were blue—as dark as the ocean's center, and as deep.

She turned away and picked out the next chair to try, settling carefully into the seat with a sigh. She looked tired, he thought, but that was no wonder. His own arms were still tingling a bit from carrying Sam around the store while Kady tried on clothes. How was she—much smaller and lighter than he—doing it?

"Much better," she said thoughtfully and shifted the baby till he rested more comfortably against her shoulder. "But then you're a lot taller than I am, and it might not be comfortable for you." She stood up and held out Sam. "Give it a try."

The baby roused with a whimper and clutched at Kady.

"I'll take your word for it," Devlin said dryly. He signalled the nearest sales clerk and asked if the chair could be delivered that afternoon.

It was not only Saturday, the clerk pointed out, but a holiday weekend... Eventually, however, Devlin prevailed.

When he turned back to Kady, still pleased with his victory, he was startled by the way she was looking at him. Her eyes had narrowed and turned almost cold— as if the woman was running calculations in the computer she fondly called her brain.

The instant she realized he was watching her, she relaxed—except, he saw, for the chill in her eyes. That remained, and so did the suspicion that had rolled over him once more like a bleak Lake Michigan fog.

Though, he admitted ruefully, she *still* had the most inviting mouth he'd ever seen.

With the rocking chair arranged for, they moved on to the children's department. A few minutes later, with Sam napping in his new stroller, they left the store and walked down the length of the mall toward the parking lot where they'd left the car. Devlin had gone completely quiet, and though he sauntered along beside the stroller it seemed to Kady that he wasn't even on the same planet as she and Sam were.

You're being unreasonable, Kady told herself. The fact that she'd fallen in love with Sam in an instant didn't mean everyone in the world should feel the same.

But how much was it going to take for Devlin to accept his son, to acknowledge him, to begin to feel an attraction for the child?

She'd had hopes, when he was carrying Sam around the store. There was something easy, almost natural, about the way he'd handled the baby's weight. And even though she'd been annoyed by the way he'd reacted to that faint *da-da*, it had been a step in the right direction.

But then he'd refused even to try rocking the baby—and Kady's heart had chilled once more. The man was still putting out negative vibes as strong as a mushroom cloud. It was no wonder the baby didn't want anything to do with Devlin. Sam had no trouble recognizing fear, uncertainty and displeasure when he ran into them, and she couldn't blame him for not wanting to get any closer.

Of course, Kady had to admit, it was easier for her. She had nothing at stake where Sam was concerned. To her, he was merely the proverbial cute baby, the sort of adorable tyke everyone clucked over and admired. There was nothing personal about her attraction.

Whereas, for Devlin, it was different. His entire life-style was at risk—threatened by a twenty-pound baby boy with a two-word vocabulary. And of course Devlin wouldn't give up everything he was used to lightly, or cheerfully.

If he gave up his pleasures at all.

Kady forced herself to consider the alternatives. None of them looked very good for Sam, she admitted. If Devlin kept the child but didn't get personally involved with his care, Sam could well grow up a lonely, wounded little boy, eternally seeking the love his father denied him. If Devlin didn't keep him, Sam would probably be caught in the trap of foster care—for unless his mother was found and gave her permission, he wouldn't be legally free for adoption. The likelihood was that he'd be moved from family to family, never feeling quite at home.

Kady was so wrapped up in that pessimistic picture she didn't even notice Devlin had disappeared. She glanced around, half-panicking, till she spotted him just inside a small corner store crammed with baseball cards and comic books.

"I should have known," she muttered as she came up beside Devlin at a display rack. "Still, you could have told me where you were going."

"I did." He didn't look up from the issue he was inspecting. "It's not my fault if you weren't listening. What were you thinking about, anyway?"

The young man behind the counter stretched his neck to what seemed impossible lengths in order to peek into the stroller. "Hey, Devlin—what's that you've got in the buggy?"

"An appetite with a tornado siren attached. Do you have the new Crime Stompers edition?"

The clerk shook his head. "Had some, but it's sold out already. I'm waiting for another shipment. Want me to hold a copy for you?"

"Why not?" Kady said under her breath. "It'll go well with the two dozen you already have."

Devlin ignored her. "No, that's fine. I was just wondering how the series was doing." He bought an old *Superman* and tucked the bag into a pocket on the back of the stroller. "You know, when Sam's asleep he's not bad to have around. And the stroller's positively handy."

"I'm glad you're coming to terms with the situation. Now if you could just manage to work up some enthusiasm for the kid himself—"

Devlin stopped in the middle of the mall, apparently unaware that he was blocking traffic. "Is *that* what's bothering you?"

"Oh, no." Kady's voice dripped irony. "I think it's simply wonderful that you're resisting the urge to get attached to him. After all, if you paid him any attention, he might get spoiled, and we wouldn't want that, would we?"

"You need some practice with out-and-out sarcasm,

Kady. You're much better when you use a rapier instead of a broadsword.''

She pushed the stroller out of the way of a very large woman wearing red-striped slacks. At least he'd noticed the mockery in her voice. That was some progress.

"You have this nice little romantic view of the universe, don't you?'' Devlin went on. "Cute baby plus devoted daddy equals happily ever after. Hasn't it occurred to you that the mother who arranged for Sam to be dropped off so casually, without even making sure I was home, might just as suddenly decide she wants him back?''

It hadn't. Kady's feelings about Sam's mother were so unprintable that she hadn't given the woman credit for any normal emotions at all. "I doubt it,'' she said tartly. "Any woman who could abandon a helpless baby like that probably won't even miss him.''

"I can think of other reasons besides maternal longing for his mother to want to reclaim him.''

"Like what?''

"For one, that Cunningham family trust fund that you're so fond of throwing in my face. If I was to get so attached to this kid that I didn't want to give him up, I might pay any amount of money to persuade his mother to disappear again. Or at least she might think I'd pay. And that's only one possibility, you understand. There are at least half a dozen other scenarios I can think of off the top of my head.''

"What did you ever see in this woman, anyway?'' Kady bit her tongue too late. "Never mind. I don't think I want to hear the answer to that.''

"Whenever I figure out who she is,'' Devlin said dryly, "I'll certainly let you know.''

CHAPTER FIVE

WHY should it bother her so much, anyway? Devlin Cunningham was a playboy whose carelessness had come home to roost. He was getting exactly what he deserved. The questions of who Sam's mother was, why Devlin had been attracted to her in the first place, why he hadn't even known about his son's existence and how many women were on that list of his...none of those things was really any of Kady's business.

But the more she told herself she was only interested in Sam's welfare, the more hollowly the questions rang in her head.

There was no doubt in her mind about why Sam's mother would have been attracted to Devlin. Kady had felt the effects of that incredible magnetic attraction of his, so she could hardly deny that another woman might have fallen into the same snare. And if that woman didn't have the benefit of Kady's experience and knowledge of how unreliable he really was...

She shook her head. She didn't want to feel compassion for Sam's mother. Any woman who could so lightly abandon her child didn't deserve sympathy. Perhaps Devlin was right, after all, in suspecting that the woman's motives were less than pure.

Still, how could any man not have a clue to the identity of his son's mother?

Which brought Kady squarely back to where she'd started, with the questions still echoing in her mind.

"Even if she does," she began.

"Even if who does what?" Devlin emerged from the back of the car, looking slightly frazzled but triumphant. "I will now accept your applause for having successfully transferred Sam into his seat without provoking either a tantrum on his part or an attack of lower back pain on mine."

"Congratulations. Of course, he's still three-fourths asleep, which certainly helps. As I was saying, even if Sam's mother wants him back—"

"Are you still thinking about that? I wondered why you went dead quiet on me." Devlin folded up the new stroller and fit it in the trunk of the car.

"Are you avoiding the subject again, Cunningham? You still won't be off the hook entirely, you know. Or hasn't it occurred to you that even if Sam gets his mother back, he'll still need a dad?"

"If we're talking in general philosophical terms about the needs of babies, I'll happily agree. But until I know a whole lot more about this specific situation, I'm not committing myself to anything."

"It's hardly Sam's fault that his mother is an idiot!"

"Yes, she appears to be. I'm glad we finally agree on something." Devlin's voice was mild.

Kady frowned. Writing off Sam's mother as a fool wasn't what she'd meant at all. The trouble was, she was no longer certain exactly what she thought where Devlin Cunningham was concerned.

They stopped at a deli for take-out sandwiches, and when they got back to the town house, Sam polished off a whole container of yogurt, a fair amount of Kady's turkey club and the rest of last night's milk. With his good humor restored by nap and nourishment, he crawled over to the row of cabinets and started excavating pots and pans and banging them together.

Devlin winced at the noise. "Maybe we should have bought more toys."

"Why? He'd still prefer the pots and pans."

He eyed her curiously. "How did you happen to learn so much about infants, Kady?"

"At Oakwood, everyone was encouraged to look after the littler ones. Since the youngest students were five and six, they weren't much more than babies, really. Then as soon as I was old enough, I started baby-sitting for some of the staff and board members."

"You didn't have enough of other kids without taking care of them in your spare time, too?"

She smiled. "What spare time? Besides, I liked having only one or two kids around, for a change."

He asked, very softly, "Was it awful, Kady?"

Why was he asking? Was he wondering what Sam would face if Devlin gave him up? She didn't want to give him a falsely positive view. While the residential school had been the best alternative she could have hoped for, considering the circumstances of her childhood, it had been a poor substitute for what she had wanted. For any child who had an alternative, it was—in Kady's opinion—unthinkable.

"Sorry if that was nosy." Devlin's voice was gentle. "I was just wondering."

She searched his face and couldn't find anything but compassion, so she shrugged and said quietly, "It worked out. But I liked escaping from there sometimes. When I took care of the staff's kids, I could earn a little money—I knew even then that college would be hard to manage. And I could also pretend for a while that I belonged somewhere—that I had my own room, my own special things. My own family." Her voice cracked.

Devlin stretched out a hand, the long tanned fingers cupped as if to cradle hers.

Kady swallowed hard. Her hand almost ached with

the desire to feel the pressure of his, the reassurance of his touch. But she didn't want him to think she was telling him a sob story purely in the hope of winning sympathy. That wasn't her reason at all. It was important that Devlin understand how lost a child could feel when he had no one who belonged to him—and how tragic it would be for Sam to be so limited when there was another choice.

But she was afraid if she tried to explain that, he'd think she sounded pathetic—and she might even start to cry. She was choked up enough as it was. So she stood and briskly began to clean up the mess from their lunch.

Devlin drew his hand back very slowly. "How did you handle it?" he asked. "College, I mean."

Kady shrugged. "Scholarships. Grants. Loans." She wondered if Devlin knew that his grandmother was the one who had funded those loans. Quite possibly he did. Though Iris talked little of her philanthropic pursuits, Kady suspected she was far from the only one who had benefited from the woman's generosity.

And just in case he knows, she thought, *let's make it clear that I don't intend to take advantage of her.* "I'll be years paying it back. That's why it's so important I get all the clients I can handle. Speaking of which, I'd still like to get some work done this weekend. So if you don't mind—"

Devlin seemed to understand that the moment for confidences was past, for the quizzical look she'd grown accustomed to reappeared in his eyes. "If you're suggesting I make my phone calls from here, with Sam's racket going on in the background..."

Kady shrugged. "You might as well get used to it. I need to check my answering service and probably get in touch with some clients."

He sighed. "Help yourself to an office upstairs. But don't be surprised if you have company anyway. I'd bet the minute Sam notices you're gone he'll be scrambling to follow you.''

"Take it as a challenge," Kady recommended. "You can practice your sales techniques on Sam—and who knows, you might like the job so well you won't bother with those phone calls, you'll just keep him."

She climbed to the main floor offices and settled into the cubicle nearest the top of the stairs, the one that Hal usually used, so she could call her apartment to check the messages on her answering machine.

Her peace and quiet lasted only five minutes, however. She was still listing her messages when Sam came into view, his little face determined as he hauled himself up the last of the flight of steps. His smile when he spotted Kady was as brilliant as if he'd just climbed through a blizzard on Mount Everest to find sunshine awaiting him at the summit.

She couldn't help smiling at him, but the way she looked at Devlin, who was only a step behind the child, wasn't nearly as warm. "You put him up to this, didn't you? I should have known."

"Cross my heart and hope to die, I didn't. It was all his own idea. That's what took him so long to get here, since he made a couple of wrong turns before he figured out where you'd gone." Devlin perched on the corner of Hal's desk and waited till she'd finished jotting down her messages. "You know, Kady, it seems to me you were right about those phone calls of mine. There isn't any sense in pursuing them."

Kady looked at him doubtfully. "I don't think I want to hear this." She picked up Sam and set him on her knee. He gleefully grabbed for her notes.

"I don't mean I'm just going to give up, you understand. But everybody who's still on my list seems to be out of town for the holiday, so it's a waste of time. And since it looks like I won't have things solved by Tuesday—''

"That," Kady said dryly, "is the first sensible thing you've said all weekend."

Devlin went straight on as if she hadn't spoken. "I'm going to need a nanny. Sam obviously wants you, and you like him just fine, too. Therefore—"

"Hold it. Hold everything! I can see this perfect plan solving your problem and Sam's, but what about me? I have a business to run, remember? I have obligations, debts—"

Devlin shrugged. "That's where my idea becomes simply brilliant. You said yourself that all your clients are small and unprofitable right now."

"I said nothing of the sort."

"You didn't?" He looked puzzled. "I could have sworn you did. But I'm your biggest account, right?"

"At the moment, yes, but—"

"See? This is the perfect answer. I'll pay you, of course, for taking care of Sam, and you can still keep up your business with just one client—me. You won't need the others, and look at the time you'll save not having to seek them out, return their calls and deal with their petty problems."

Kady stared at him openmouthed. The man sounded absolutely serious.

"It won't be forever, anyway," Devlin went on blithely. "Sooner or later Sam's mother is bound to be in touch. And even if it's only a matter of days, you'll still be better off, because you'll be rid of your unprofitable clients, and I'll keep that promise I made to get you some bigger ones."

Kady ignored him and started to dial the first number on her list of messages. It seemed the safest thing to do, since the alternative was to scream—and the chances were if she started to yell at Devlin Cunningham about how inconsiderate, how irresponsible and how annoying he was, she'd never manage to stop.

She hadn't taken the bait. Devlin hadn't expected that she'd leap at it, of course——Kady Bishop was too intelligent to rise to a lure without thinking it over. But he'd been sure she would ask for a chance to consider his offer and then ultimately accept the job as Sam's nanny. After all, the proposition made a great deal of sense where she was concerned—in all kinds of ways.

But she'd turned it down flat. So at least he knew for certain that she wasn't trying to insinuate herself into his life. If she'd had any such intentions, she'd have dangled him by a thread for a while and let him think she was seriously considering his offer. And she would probably have let him hold her hand, too, and maybe even allowed him to blot a tear or two from those gorgeous blue-green eyes of hers.

Instead, she'd pulled away as if he was the bearer of a contagious disease.

Well, fine, he thought. At least he'd found out that much.

Still, the possibility remained that—with or without Kady's connivance—he was being set up for blackmail. Saddle him with a kid, wait for his frustration level to blow a gasket and then offer to take Sam off his hands…for a price, of course. Well, he'd just have to wait and see. If that was what was going on, he'd know soon enough.

Sam babbled and grinned and tried to snatch the telephone from Kady's hand. She took a firmer grip, and the baby looked at her with mischief in his gaze and delicately fingered the numbered push buttons on the phone. Devlin could hear the dissonant notes even from five feet away. He could imagine what the noise was like from where Kady sat.

Sam was a cute kid, that was hard to deny, with those big, dark eyes and the blond corkscrew curls. Beyond the color of their eyes and hair, though, Devlin was darned if he could see the resemblance between the two of them that seemed so apparent to Kady.

She snuggled the receiver under her chin and pushed the telephone base out of Sam's reach. "Quite a musician, isn't he?" she said with a laugh. "No, I'm just sort of baby-sitting." She paused. "Oh, I'm sorry, but I can't. Maybe next week, though. All right, I'll see you there."

Who was she talking to, anyway? Devlin wondered. Surely it wasn't a client. That had hardly been a businesslike laugh. From the soft look in her eyes, it was obviously a man. Was this the person she'd been thinking of earlier today when she'd said, "Men can be incredibly..." and stopped?

Incredibly *what*? Devlin mused. Nothing pleasant, that was sure—which probably meant this wasn't the same man, or she wouldn't be acting so lighthearted now.

And what was it she couldn't do for this unknown man? Maybe he'd left a message for her asking for a date tonight. If so, if he had waited so late to call, it served him right to find she already had plans for the evening. Even if they weren't quite the sort of plans an attractive young woman usually made for a Saturday night...

Devlin frowned. Maybe he should do something about that. Just because she was helping him out was no reason she should miss all the fun.

He wondered where she'd agreed to meet the guy.

And he wondered if the man knew that Kady Bishop wore a red lace bra under those tailored suits of hers.

By the time Kady finished phoning all the clients who had left messages and found in her computer files the

tax data that one of them desperately needed, late afternoon sunlight was spilling through the big windows at
the back of the town house.

For the second time, Sam had cleared off Hal's desk,
dumping almost everything in the nearest wastebasket.
It took Kady fifteen minutes to straighten out the mess
and longer yet to find the snapshots of Hal's bikini-clad
girlfriends that had been tacked to the front of his desk
with magnets. Sam had hidden them in a drawer, neatly
tucking them into a file marked Things to Do.

"I'd like to know what was behind that move, Sam,"
Kady speculated. "Was it pure coincidence that you put
them in the category of unfinished business, or have you
already picked up a few ideas from your daddy?"

Sam giggled and held out his arms to be picked up.

She hadn't seen Devlin for the better part of an hour,
since he'd poked his head in the door to announce that
the rocking chair had arrived and to ask where she
wanted it. She had to give him some credit, though. Before that, he'd appeared every half hour or so to see if
he could take Sam off her hands. Each time, however,
the little boy had firmly shaken his head, said "No!" at
the top of his lungs and clung to Kady till it would have
taken dynamite to pry him loose. Finally Devlin had
given up—and Kady couldn't exactly blame him.

The aroma of some wonderful dish greeted her as she
came down to the kitchen. Sam smelled it, too, and
started to whimper.

"Are you hungry?" Kady asked him.

Sam didn't answer, but Devlin did. "Starving," he
called.

"I wasn't talking to you."

"Well, don't bother to ask Sam. Or hadn't you noticed that he feels hungry any time he sees or smells
food? It must be a Pavlovian response." Devlin ap-

peared in the door between kitchen and hallway just as Kady reached the bottom of the stairs.

He'd wrapped a dish towel around his waist, and one long hand held a gleaming carving knife. The towel made him look taller than ever before and drew attention to the perfect wedge of his body from broad shoulders to slim hips. And he was smiling, a slow, sexy and fearfully attractive smile.

The man was as dangerous as a carload of nitroglycerine, Kady thought. In fact, ounce for ounce, he was probably even more so.

And don't you forget it, she ordered herself.

"What a transformation," she said. Despite herself, her voice was a bit unsteady. She hoped he wouldn't notice. "All you need is a chef's hat and you'd be in business."

Devlin shook his head. "Don't give me too much credit. I carve a mean prime rib, but I wouldn't begin to know how to cook one. My favorite recipe begins, 'Combine one telephone and one list of restaurants...'"

Kady laughed.

He bowed with a theatrical flair. "Dinner is served. It's about time you came out of that cubbyhole of yours. I'd have come and gotten you when the prime rib arrived, but I was afraid you weren't finished yet."

"I wasn't. I'd probably have bitten you if you'd barged in at the wrong moment." He'd been right about one thing, she had to admit—petty problems took up far more of her time than she could afford. She'd spent the entire afternoon dealing with four clients, but she wouldn't dare bill them for even half the value of her time or she'd lose them entirely. They couldn't afford the true cost of her services, but she couldn't lightly give up the income they represented.

Unless, of course, she could replace them with larger, more profitable accounts. With or without Devlin's help.

"Oh, really?" Devlin murmured. "What kind of a bite? That might have been very interesting."

The soft, sensual growl in his voice made Kady forget about clients altogether to think instead of a long, warm afternoon and a gentle savanna breeze and a pair of lions indulging in a lazy bit of loving.

And that, she told herself, *is plenty of that!*

He was grinning, she saw, and she wondered uneasily if he'd read her mind.

But he said, "The prime rib started out rare, but that was half an hour ago. I hope it isn't too well-done for your taste."

"I'm sure it will be fine. Can I set the table or anything?"

Devlin shook his head. "It's all ready."

The kitchen was as neat as she had ever seen it, and the table gleamed with cutlery, bright colored napkins and stoneware dishes. The plates even matched, which startled her.

Though, Kady told herself, service for two—no more, no less—was exactly what she should have expected Devlin to own!

From hidden stereo speakers, a soft blues number filled the air as comfortingly as did the aroma of the beef, and Kady could feel the tension draining out of her as she settled Sam in his chair.

The baby twisted around, not so much trying to avoid the bib she was attempting to tie round his neck as to see what Devlin was dishing up.

"At least he's got a healthy appetite," Kady murmured. "Of course, in another few years, he'll be mopping up the last of one meal and asking with his mouth still full when the next one will be ready. Kids are like that."

"I remember. Along about the time I was thirteen, I was always hungry."

"Of course, you could probably just walk to the kitchen and do something about it, too," Kady said absently.

He stopped in mid-motion. "Do you mean you couldn't?"

"Think about it, Devlin. There were more than a hundred of us. If there hadn't been controls, there would have been a line of kids in front of the refrigerator around the clock." She caught the shocked look in his eyes and added, "I don't mean to say it was like something out of *Oliver Twist*. We had plenty to eat. It was just provided on schedule."

Devlin's carving knife sliced slowly through the rich prime rib, and a moment later he set a plate in front of her. "Enjoy," he said quietly.

She looked at the plate. The slab of beef was pink and perfect, and a baked potato and a pile of brilliant green beans steamed gently alongside.

"I think I like your favorite recipe," she admitted.

Devlin poured juice for dipping into two small dishes and set one beside her. "I forgot to ask. Is the music all right? I can put on some jazz if you'd rather."

"No, it's great."

"And what about Sam? Yogurt again?"

She glanced at the baby, who was staring at her prime rib with covetous eyes. "If there's another plate, I'll dice some of this for him. Just a minute, Sam—take it easy, all right?"

Devlin got a plate. "You don't have to share. There's more."

"How much do you think I can eat, anyway?" She started to chop up a corner of her prime rib.

A moment later Devlin put a glass of wine at her elbow.

Kady eyed the deep red liquid. The last time she'd seen it was yesterday, when Shelle had been waving the bottle around and looking for a corkscrew. She considered asking Devlin if Shelle would mind, and then thought better of it. In this incredible household, it was hard to tell who owned what. The wine probably hadn't belonged to Shelle in the first place, and even if it did, Kady had no room to talk.

"We'll have to hit a supermarket sometime so we can restock the refrigerator," she pointed out, "before the owner of all that yogurt—whoever it is—finds out that I've fed most of it to Sam. And I still have to stop by my apartment, too. I completely forgot about shoes, and I can hardly go to the picnic tomorrow like this." She held out a slim, bare foot.

Devlin shrugged. "I thought perhaps you'd like to take in a movie tonight. We can stop on the way."

He'd mellowed, Kady thought, and her forehead wrinkled a little in puzzlement over the change. Perhaps it had just taken him a while to get used to the idea of Sam, and now that he'd had a chance to adjust… Come to think of it, he'd seemed quite interested this afternoon, even eager to get closer to the baby.

Though, her suspicious brain reminded, he'd been pretty safe in taking that approach. Considering the way Sam reacted to him, Devlin wouldn't have had to be a genius to figure out that he could look concerned and caring and still not get stuck with the kid.

"Hello?" Devlin said mildly.

"Oh—sorry. Depends on what the movie is, I think. Sam's not my first choice of company for something like that. He isn't likely to sit still for long." She glanced at the baby, who had a green bean in one hand, a sticky spoon in the other and a smear of potato on the tip of his nose. From all indications, nothing had yet made it into his mouth.

Devlin cut a bit of beef and offered it to him, and Sam eagerly opened his mouth wide. "Good, isn't it?" Devlin murmured. "Of course, you have to learn to savor the taste and texture instead of gulping it like a savage."

Sam giggled.

Devlin gave the baby another bite and picked up his wineglass. Sam, intrigued by the bright color, spat out the meat and made a grab for the glass instead.

"No—believe me, that's a sensual experience you aren't ready for," Devlin said firmly. "Content yourself with the prime rib. It will almost melt in your mouth if you let it." He picked up the bit Sam had discarded from his bib, and the baby leaned forward and nipped it from Devlin's fingertip.

Kady was watching, fascinated. That was the secret, she thought. If Devlin was the only one to feed Sam, they'd soon make friends. They'd be bound to.

"Hey, take it easy," Devlin complained. "My finger isn't on the menu—for you, at least."

Sam gave a throaty chuckle.

Devlin hadn't even looked at her, but Kady felt the tingle of warm blood rising to her face nevertheless as she remembered her idle threat to bite him. She told herself that it was absolute insanity to sit there wondering how his skin would taste—but once the idea had crept across her mind, she couldn't seem to stop herself from thinking about it. Salty? Sweet? Melt-in-the-mouth delicious, just like the prime rib?

And why was it that she had no trouble at all visualizing Devlin tasting her skin, as well? She could feel the warmth and wetness of his tongue....

Hastily, she cut another bite of meat and almost choked herself by eating it too quickly. She reached for her wineglass and had lifted it halfway to her mouth when the back door opened.

Hal, she thought with resignation. Well, at least she was adequately dressed this time.

But it wasn't Hal who stood in the doorway, eyes

wide and mouth ajar. It was Shelle Emerson, her red hair perfectly coiffed and her skirt both shorter and tighter than any Kady had seen her wearing before.

"I tried to call you earlier, Devlin," Shelle said. Her voice was mechanical. Kady thought she'd probably rehearsed the line. "But nobody answered. I thought maybe there was a problem, so I thought I should stop before I went out for the evening, in case something was..." Her voice trailed off, like a battery-powered toy that had exhausted its energy. "I mean, you did say you'd call me, Devlin."

"But I didn't promise when it would be," Devlin said. His voice was almost gentle.

Shelle's gaze slid slowly from Devlin to Kady and then focused on the child. Confusion warred with disbelief in her eyes. Kady almost felt sorry for her.

Sam gave a crow of laughter and slapped his spoon into the lump of potato on his plate. White flecks flew through the air, splattering Kady's wineglass and Devlin's face.

Devlin blinked and wiped a bit out of his eyelashes. "And as you can see," he said dryly, "I'm a bit busy at the moment. Sorry if you were sitting at home waiting to hear from me, Shelle."

Shelle put a hand on her hip. "Where'd the baby come from, anyway?"

"I bought a bunch of comic books and discovered too late that he was part of the package." Devlin's voice was deadpan.

Shelle rolled her eyes. "No, really. I suppose this was your idea, Kady?"

"Not guilty. I'm just the innocent bystander, and if I hadn't happened to be the last one out the door last night, *you* might have had the pleasure."

Shelle made a sound that was almost a snort. She

wheeled around, her mass of hair slashing the air like a cleaver, and stomped out the door.

"Well," Kady said thoughtfully, "I believe that means you can mark Shelle off your list."

Devlin frowned. "She was never on it."

"Oh, I didn't mean *that* list," she assured him. "I meant your file of prospective nannies. Somehow I don't think Shelle wants the job any more than I do."

Sam banged his spoon again, and laughed.

"And by the way," Kady added sweetly, "you have potato in your eyebrow."

Devlin swore under his breath. The sound was music to her ears.

CHAPTER SIX

DEVLIN could have cheerfully dumped Shelle Emerson in the precise center of Lake Michigan and left her there. He'd been making progress till she showed up. He could feel it, though heaven knew he didn't have much real evidence to show for all the effort—just a gut feeling that an off-balance Kady Bishop would turn out to be very interesting. And she'd been off balance, as tipsy as if she'd consumed the whole bottle of wine instead of a modest half glass.

Then Shelle had walked in, and suddenly the soft and sensual side of Kady he'd begun to glimpse was gone. She had turned into an accountant again, all logic and good sense, with a veneer of sarcasm added.

Maybe, he thought, she had a point about letting his employees have the run of the town house. It had never bothered him before, but this weekend the interruptions had been major inconveniences. Left alone tonight, he might have accomplished all sorts of things.

Not seduction, of course. As inviting as the idea might be, all the logical arguments against sleeping with Kady Bishop were still just as valid.

And not the movie, either. While it had seemed a good plan at the time, Kady was right about Sam. He wasn't Devlin's first choice of company for a double feature. And he supposed a baby-sitter was out of the question. Not only didn't he have the vaguest idea where to begin seeking one out, he knew it would be a massive mistake to let Kady get the idea that Sam could continue to exist without her. No, they were a threesome for the weekend. Beyond that...

When Kady went home, he admitted with foreboding, he was going to be in very deep water.

It seemed to Devlin the old wives' tale that said the surest way to a man's heart was through his stomach was dead wrong. All a woman really had to do was offer to look after the kids, and the man in question would turn into a pathetically grateful marshmallow who'd give her anything in his power. No wonder, he thought wryly, so many men of previous generations had married multiple times. It wasn't the joys of matrimony that had attracted them, but the idea of someone else taking care of the children.

He didn't realize how silent the room had grown until Kady's chair scraped across the floor as she rose to dampen a washcloth. Then Devlin was surprised to see that his plate was empty. He'd mechanically finished his dinner without even noticing the taste.

He pushed the plate away and watched as she washed potato off Sam's face over the baby's protests.

She looked tired, he thought. There were shadows under her eyes, and she'd pushed her hair back carelessly behind her ears. He'd never seen it so untidy before—though it still gleamed blue-black in the harsh kitchen light, and its softness seemed to entice him to smooth it with the palm of his hand.

"Maybe you and I should try out the new rocking chair instead of the movies, Sam," Kady said, and yawned.

Devlin stood and lifted Sam out of her arms, ignoring the child's strenuous objections. The move surprised him, and—judging by the look on Kady's face—stunned her to the point of paralysis.

He was almost annoyed. Did she honestly think he

was so hopelessly selfish as not even to have noticed the strain she'd been under all day?

"Maybe," he said, "you should forget the rocking chair altogether and try out something even more relaxing."

"What have you got in mind?"

He was watching her face, so he knew the instant she heard the double meaning in her words. His annoyance vanished, and delight spread through him as thoroughly as hot color raced over her. Maybe, he thought, Shelle hadn't been as big an interruption as he'd thought. If a comment no more suggestive than *that* could have such a tremendous effect on Kady...

"Like a long soak in a hot tub," he said deliberately. "Alone, while Sam and I entertain each other. Why? What did you think I meant?"

She wouldn't look at him, but that didn't concern Devlin. His good spirits had returned. There would be time. He had the rest of the weekend, after all.

Unless, of course, the inconvenient and tiresome woman who'd dropped Sam off turned up again. The moment she surfaced, Kady would be gone.

Perhaps, Devlin mused, he wasn't in such a hurry for her to reappear, after all.

The tub was luxurious. The black marble seemed to have been carved to cradle Kady's body. The water was satiny soft with bubble bath, and the whirlpool jets flung it against her skin with just the right amount of force to pummel her body into relaxation.

The scented water was a potent formula, mixed as it was with sheer exhaustion and the ache of muscles no longer used to hefting twenty pounds of small boy on a regular basis.

She sank deeper into the water so the jets could pound against her shoulders, her neck, her scalp.

The machinery was surprisingly quiet. The jets hissed rather than roared, as she'd expected they would. When she surfaced, her hair dripping, she could hear Sam crying in the bedroom next door, and her heart twisted.

The poor little guy was sobbing pitifully. No wonder, she thought. He believed he'd been abandoned again, and he didn't understand—how could he? He'd suffered so many changes in such a short time. New people surrounded him, people who didn't seem to understand what he wanted or know what he was used to. He was in an entirely new place, with a new bed, new clothes, even a new stuffed animal to hug instead of an old, comfortable friend. And now even the one person he'd turned to for consolation was gone. It must seem to him that he was caught in a nightmare.

She should do something about it. If she went to him, he'd at least stop crying.

No, she told herself. Devlin and Sam were going to have to strike a deal sooner or later—and the fact was, the faster they came to an understanding, the better for both of them. Her only responsibility in this mess was to ease the transition, making sure Devlin had the knowledge he needed, reassuring Sam that he could trust Devlin. But the more she interfered the harder it would be for both of them.

She would concentrate on the positive, she told herself. It was wonderful that Devlin suddenly seemed determined to break through Sam's resistance and take a real part in his care. Of course, he still hadn't admitted Sam was his baby—but surely that was only a matter of time.

Maybe she'd underestimated the effectiveness of the child's charm when it came to winning Devlin over. Or maybe she'd underestimated Devlin himself. Perhaps he was going to end up being a caring parent, after all, once he'd had a few days to adjust to the shock. At least, with his quirky business pursuits, he'd have more time for the child than many single parents did.

Now if Sam could just be persuaded to give him a chance…

The cries had faded to an occasional whimper, and the knot in Kady's stomach loosened a little. She sank back in the water again.

They were going to make it, this unlikely combination of father and son, she told herself reassuringly.

So why wasn't she thrilled by the knowledge?

Devlin could hear the faint roar of the water jets even over Sam's screams. Funny, he thought. He'd never realized before what an erotic sound that was. Of course, he had to admit, this was the first time he'd sat in his bedroom and listened to the whirlpool, drawing pictures in his mind of what was going on in his bathroom.

He could see Kady, leaning back in the bubbles with one slim leg lifted out of the water, her bare foot arched, drops of water sliding down the sole and dripping from the heel….

He had as clear an image of that slender bare foot as if he'd studied it under a microscope for hours instead of eyeing it for something short of ten seconds under the edge of the kitchen table.

And as for the rest of her, he had no more trouble imagining that than he did her foot. Slim, straight shoulders. Skin the color of rich cream, flushed slightly pink by the warm water. Well-defined bones, strong but delicately made, that begged to be traced by a man's fingertip. Slender arms, nicely rounded breasts…

Perhaps it was just as well, he told himself, that keeping Sam under control took the majority of his attention, or he'd have an even more difficult time staying on the sensible side of that firmly closed door.

Sam appeared, unaccountably, to be in a much better

mood all of a sudden. "Are you giving me a break?" Devlin murmured. "I didn't know you had it in you."

Sam gave a fleeting, enigmatic grin.

Devlin smiled—he *was* a cute kid—then sniffed and looked suspiciously at the child.

He tossed a longing look toward the bathroom, but now that Kady was enjoying the whirlpool, he suspected nothing short of a fire alarm going off would make her open that door. In fact, he thought dryly, even that might not pry her from the tub, because—suspicious as she was—she'd probably think he'd set it off deliberately.

"Whose dumb idea was it for her to soak in the tub anyway, Cunningham?" he muttered.

Sam wrinkled his nose and looked thoughtful.

"Easy for you to feel philosophical," Devlin told him. "Your part of the hard work's done."

He could knock on the door, of course, and ask her to come out and give him a hand. But she needed the relaxation. Besides, he didn't exactly want to hear what she'd have to say about it if he interrupted her bath to deal with this. She'd no doubt mutter something about incompetence and cowardice....

He'd watched Kady change Sam. She'd even insisted that he take his turn, and he'd managed just fine, considering that he'd never seen a disposable diaper before this weekend. But a wet kid was a whole different proposition than a dirty one.

Sam yelled throughout the process, and Devlin wanted to. It was an ordeal that left them both exhausted and Sam tear-drenched. But Devlin's ultimate triumph left him feeling that he could do anything. He could scale mountains, he could slay dragons, he could end the world's injustice...and maybe he could even rock Sam to sleep.

The rocking chair was darned uncomfortable, and he'd sat in it only a couple of minutes, with a wriggling

Sam in his arms, before he regretted not taking Kady's advice in the store and trying it out himself. She'd looked downright comfortable sitting in it this morning. So what was wrong with him? He was taller, of course—but his discomfort was caused by more than mere height. His elbows seemed to stick out at the wrong angles, and every time he rocked, his spine rattled against the chair's back.

He shifted uneasily. Sam whimpered a sleepy protest and reached for something on the floor beside the chair. Devlin craned his neck to see what it was, and stretched to retrieve the stuffed giraffe. Sam hugged the animal close, put his face against Devlin's neck and abruptly sagged like a sack of wet rice. Devlin could twist his head just enough to see the child's face, innocent and angelic, with dark-tipped eyelashes resting heavily on his cheekbones.

"Oh, now that's fiendish," he complained under his breath. "I'm in the most uncomfortable position I've ever assumed in my life, and now I can't move for fear I'll wake you up!"

Distraction—that was the key. He'd concentrate so completely on something else that he'd forget all about his discomfort. It had worked on the last long-distance race he'd run—he'd simply pretended to be jogging through Regent's Park, and before he knew it he'd run through the pain and had his second wind.

What to think about was the problem. The image of Kady in the whirlpool would be plenty distracting—he could envision her eyelashes clumped in damp spikes, her hair trailing in wet tendrils around those soft shoulders—but that kind of visualization was likely only to make him more uncomfortable. Perhaps if he thought of her in the rocking chair with Sam and how at ease she'd seemed to be...

What a sight they had made, sitting together in the

store this morning, with Sam drowsing in her arms—like a Madonna and child. Devlin hadn't realized till now that he'd so clearly noted the striking contrast between her dark hair and Sam's bright curls, between the angular lines of Kady's slender face and the baby's chubby cheeks, between her enormous wide eyes and the child's, closed as he rested so trustingly in her arms. Between the childishly rounded lines of the baby's body and the slim, suggestive, womanly curves of Kady's. The memory was so clear that even now Devlin's palm itched to stroke the soft swell of Kady's breast.

He closed his eyes and drew a picture in his mind—and forgot about the ache in his spine.

When the timer ran out and shut the water jets off, Kady opened her eyes reluctantly and considered giving the dial another twist. But she couldn't stay in forever, however much she'd like to. The soles of her feet already looked like prunes.

And besides, the bedroom was almost threateningly silent. She wouldn't put it past Devlin to have taken Sam out for a car ride in the hope of putting him to sleep. Still, curiosity impelled her to check.

She wrapped her hair in a towel and herself in Devlin's brocade robe and quietly opened the bathroom door.

The bedroom was dim, but light from the hallway spilled across the back of the rocking chair, where two golden heads lay close together.

Kady tiptoed closer. Two pairs of dark, silky eyelashes resting heavily on high, firm cheekbones... Two quiet breathing patterns that sounded almost like one...

Her heart swelled with quiet pride. She wasn't sure if she was prouder of Devlin for making the try or Sam for cooperating. All she knew was that she wanted, at this moment, to hug them both.

Without conscious decision, her hand went out—though she wasn't sure if she intended to touch Devlin's silky hair or caress Sam's curls.

She never found out, for Devlin jerked upright, eyes suddenly wide. Kady jumped a foot, and Sam started to cry.

"I'm sorry," she stammered. "I thought you were both asleep."

"I might have dozed. I certainly didn't hear the tub shut off." He looked at the baby, who was shrieking and holding up his arms to Kady. "I thought we were doing better, Sam," he said sadly, "and then you turn on me like this."

Sam's face crumpled into a blur, and he wailed louder. Devlin shrugged and handed him over.

"Don't feel too bad about it," Kady said as she cuddled Sam close. "It's really no wonder he's more comfortable with women."

"If you're trying to make me feel better about what was clearly a personal rejection, Kady, don't bother." He got out of the rocking chair and stretched.

"No, really. If there's never been a man present in his life—"

"How do you know there hasn't?"

Kady rolled her eyes. "I assumed since you'd never seen him till this weekend—"

"That there couldn't possibly be a man hanging around his mother? That's a mighty big assumption, don't you think?"

Kady was taken aback. But Devlin was right, she realized. The kind of woman who would so lightly abandon her child would hardly be the sort to live like a nun. If her relationship with her baby's father broke down, she might well have taken up with another man—or even several in succession.

Though Kady couldn't quite see what any woman

could find appealing about another man after she'd once been attracted to Devlin.

Wait a minute, she told herself. That thought hadn't come out quite the way she'd meant it.

"What are you frowning about?" Devlin asked.

Kady had to scramble for an answer. "I was just thinking about the note she pinned to Sam's shirt. She didn't say anything about another man."

"That doesn't mean there isn't one. Though at the moment it seems a pointless exercise to speculate about it." His gaze slid slowly over her, from damp hair to heat-pinkened toes.

Kady's heart fluttered a little. *It's embarrassment*, she told herself. She hadn't stopped to think, before she plunged out of the bathroom, that she wasn't properly attired for the occasion.

"That smoking jacket looks a lot better on you than it ever did on me," Devlin said matter-of-factly.

Kady's heartbeat slowed to normal. In fact, there was an odd empty feeling in the pit of her stomach. Was it disappointment? *Don't be ridiculous*, she ordered herself. *You don't want him to be attracted to you. You're relieved that he isn't.*

She shifted her hold on Sam and noticed the way the heavy brocade rustled as she moved. The lush, sensual sound was mimicked by the slick smoothness shifting against her skin. "I was surprised to find it. It somehow didn't seem like the kind of thing you'd have."

Devlin shrugged. "It's a relic of a play I was in years ago, in college. I'd forgotten it was still at the back of my closet."

"You were interested in drama?"

"Isn't everyone, in our foolish and feckless youth?"

"I don't know," Kady said simply. "I was always too busy studying, trying to keep my grades up. And we didn't have much in the way of extras at Oakwood. A few sports, because the exercise was good for us. Some music, since a couple of the patrons donated old instruments and gave lessons. But a drama department is pretty expensive to run.''

He was silent, and after a moment Kady realized how she must have sounded—a bit pitiful, as if she was asking for sympathy. *Idiot*, she told herself. She looked at Sam, who'd settled close against her, and said softly, ''I think he's drowsy enough to drop off to sleep, so I'm going to put him down while he's still alert enough to know where he is.''

''Why?'' Devlin asked. ''If he's almost asleep, why take the chance on waking him up all over again?''

''Because that was the mistake I made last night—he was sound asleep when I put him in bed, and when he roused he didn't recognize anything, so he was frightened.''

''Oh. I suppose that's logical.''

''Of course it is. I'll bet when you wake up in a different bed, you're—'' Hot color surged over her. ''Never mind.'' She tried to ignore his half-smile. If Devlin wanted to dwell on pleasant memories she'd accidentally brought to mind, that was his business, but she had absolutely no interest in tallying up the number of beds he'd occupied, or how he felt upon awakening in a strange one.

She went on firmly, ''We shouldn't be in the same room with Sam, or he won't settle down. But we need to be close enough to hear if he needs reassuring.''

''So what do we do? Sit at the top of the stairway?''

''What about your study?''

''It's no more comfortable than the stairs, believe me.''

''I'm sure it'll do.'' She put Sam on his stomach in the crib, tucked the stuffed giraffe next to him and leaned over the rail to pat his back and sing him to sleep.

She was terribly aware of Devlin lounging in the doorway, and she felt relieved when he finally turned away and strolled down the hall.

She stayed beside Sam till his eyes fluttered shut and hovered a little longer till she was sure he was sound asleep. Then, reluctantly, she followed Devlin down the hall.

He was standing beside the desk, a file drawer open, slipping papers into folders. When Kady came in, he nudged the drawer shut with his knee and gestured at the wooden swivel chair next to the desk. "It's the most comfortable one—but I'm afraid that isn't saying much."

She took the chair, and Devlin tugged a tall stool away from a nearby drawing board and perched on it.

Kady looked around as unobtrusively as she could. She would have expected the bedroom to be the most personal room in his private quarters, or perhaps the bath. But apart from the stereo system and the toilet articles, there was little about those rooms to distinguish them from an upscale hotel.

This room, however, was different. She sensed that this was where Devlin really came to life.

Stacks of comic books occupied the floor, as if he'd been sorting out one of the private collections he was forever buying. One of the inventory sheets she'd devised in the first week she'd worked for him lay nearby. It was as pristine as the day it had been printed.

So much for that effort to organize him, she thought.

The drawing board was empty, but probably only because it was set at the highest angle and so was too steep a surface to hold more than a single sheet of paper. The surface of the desk was cluttered with letters, trade newspapers and more comic books. In the center of the desk blotter was the note that had been pinned to Sam's shirt.

Kady picked it up. All the handwriting was cramped and hard to read, but the signature was impossible.

"Do you suppose she did it on purpose?" she mused.

Devlin had picked up an eraser and was idly rubbing out a mark on the drawing board. "What are you talking about?"

"Scrawling her name this way. Maybe she doesn't *want* to be found."

"The thought had occurred to me. The signature doesn't ring any bells with you?"

"Why should it? You surely don't think *I* try to keep a list of your women? In any case, what good would it do if I did keep track? I haven't been around nearly long enough to have known her—whoever she was. If Sam's a year old, give or take, and you never even knew she was pregnant, that means she was gone long before I came to work."

"There is that problem, of course," he said idly. "But it was worth a try. Thanks for the compliment, by the way."

Kady frowned. "What compliment?"

"You seemed to be implying that if I *had* known anything about a pregnancy, things would be very different. That's a considerable improvement from the sort of thing you were accusing me of yesterday."

Kady had to stop and consider. She had no trouble recalling some of the things she'd said last night. She no longer felt quite so vehement—but had she really changed her mind about him?

I hope you'll be more reliable for him than you were for me, Sam's mother had written. She must have had reason to say that. And yet, Kady couldn't quite make herself believe that the unreliability the woman spoke of had anything to do with Sam or with her pregnancy. If Devlin had known about the child, why would he deny that fact to Kady—who didn't matter a pin to him?

Because I might tell his grandmother, she thought.

But that reasoning didn't hold water, either. Devlin was not only a grown man, but a very self-assured one. This episode wouldn't be the first time Iris Cunningham had been livid about his behavior, and he'd probably react the same way he had those other times, with a raised eyebrow and a jesting comment. He might, she thought, try to soften the blow out of respect for his grandmother—but Devlin wasn't such a coward as to lie about anything he'd done.

And he wouldn't have run from his responsibility to his child, either, or to the mother of that child, if he'd known. He might not have married the woman—but he wouldn't have turned his back on her.

Good heavens, Kady thought. *I'd better watch out, or I'll find myself actually defending the man!*

"You're welcome, I guess," she said, with a shrug. Before he could pursue the subject—if, indeed, he'd want to—she picked up the note again and turned the paper sideways. "It's not a long name," she observed. "That might help. Six or seven letters, I'd say, and the first one might be an *M*. On the other hand, it could well be a nickname."

"Or even an assumed name, if she's trying to hide."

Kady nodded. "In either case, trying to make sense out of it would be futile."

"You're such a positive thinker, my dear."

Kady was barely listening. "Maybe the other man in her life doesn't want a baby," she speculated.

"And maybe you're building houses on quicksand."

"What's that supposed to mean?"

"That your conclusions can't possibly be valid when you're starting with supposed facts that may turn out not be true."

"Oh, come on, Devlin. It doesn't take much brain-power to figure out the 'supposed facts.'"

"I know—anyone with the intelligence of a dustpan can do it. Just go on entertaining yourself and forget I objected, all right?"

He sounded positively curt. Kady started to put the note down. On the blotter where it had been lying was Devlin's list. About a dozen names had been scratched off it, but better than twice that many remained.

Three dozen women? Kady thought. *And he accused me of making him sound like Casanova?* "Well, there isn't any need to be rude about it," she said sweetly. "If you're anxious to get on with your calls, go ahead. I don't mind."

"It's a little late, don't you think?"

About a year and a half too late, she wanted to say. But she bit her tongue. There was nothing to be gained by sniping. The whole question of Sam wasn't anything to her, anyway. If she jabbed Devlin about it, she'd only make him irritable, which would probably upset the baby. And she might even end up looking like she cared—as if she was jealous of the women in his life. Which, of course, was utterly ridiculous.

In any case, he must have simply meant the hour. She glanced at the clock. It *was* past ten—but surely Devlin's type wouldn't be tucked into their beds just yet.

At least, not alone, she thought, and winced. Just when had she become so incredibly catty?

Maybe he just meant that the women he knew wouldn't be home sitting beside their telephones on a Saturday night at this hour. That was far more likely, Kady told herself.

She yawned. "You know, I think Sam's all settled. And frankly, since I've had a very long day myself, I think I'll go to bed."

Devlin picked up the eraser again. "I'd been meaning to mention that."

"What about it? If you want to take me home, I'm all for it, but—"

"What if Sam wakes up?" He shook his head. "No, I just meant we need an arrangement a little better than last night's."

"Why? Where did you sleep last night?"

"In the chair you're occupying."

"Oh," Kady said uncertainly.

"I'm sure you've noticed that it's not going to win any prizes for comfort."

"If you think I'm going to share your bed..." She stammered to a halt, feeling foolish. It was, after all, *his* bed—she'd pointed the fact out herself.

"I certainly wasn't campaigning to evict you. But I hope you don't mind if I toss a couple of blankets on the floor."

"You mean, in the bedroom?"

Devlin nodded and added patiently, "There's nowhere else with enough space for me to stretch out."

Kady felt like a fool for asking. It was obvious he couldn't sleep on the study floor unless he turned the stacks of comic books into a mattress. The rooms downstairs were too full of desks and shelves and filing cabinets to leave room for him to stretch out. And the hallway had a wooden floor—hardly the most comfortable place for a makeshift bed.

And why was she so upset at the idea, anyway? She'd been sitting around in a robe for the last hour, and he hadn't attacked her. What would be so different about going to sleep in the same room? She couldn't be safer. Even when she'd offered him the opening of a lifetime with that remark about sharing his bed, he hadn't jumped on it and tried to convince her that it was large enough for both of them. Which obviously meant the idea of sleeping with her held no attraction at all for Devlin.

She shrugged. "Suit yourself. Though if you're looking for sheer space to stretch out, you might try the bathtub—it's plenty big.''

"What's the matter, Kady? Did you feel lonely in there all by yourself?''

"No," Kady said between her teeth. "And I'm certainly not inviting you to keep me company next time, either.''

Devlin's laugh was low and warm and full of pure amusement, as if the idea was so ridiculous it was entertaining.

Kady wanted to hit him. She'd have slammed the bedroom door, but the sound would have awakened Sam.

So she slid between Devlin's sheets and curled up with her back to him, trying not to listen as he rustled around the room, arranging his bed.

And trying not to wonder why he wasn't the slightest bit attracted to her. What was there about her—Kady Bishop—that turned him off so completely he preferred a blanket on the floor and laughed at the idea of sharing that sensuous whirlpool with her?

She told herself it didn't matter. But her heart was full of bleakness nonetheless.

CHAPTER SEVEN

A BLANKET on the bedroom floor was slightly softer than the swivel chair beside his desk had been, but that was all Devlin could say for it. It wasn't much of an improvement in other ways, he concluded as he twisted restlessly on his makeshift bed.

At least last night, when he'd practically passed out from exhaustion in his study, he hadn't been able to hear the rustle of linen as Kady turned over in his bed, and he hadn't found pictures floating through his brain as he imagined her lying there.

Last night he'd had a great deal less information with which to torment himself, as well. He hadn't yet seen her curled up in that very bed, with Sam and the stuffed giraffe snuggled next to her. He hadn't yet seen those incredible legs, or the curve of her spine as she bent over the crib to soothe the child to sleep. Or the careless way she'd swept her hair up in a twist after her bath, leaving damp tendrils falling loose around her face, begging to be tucked into place...

She stirred again, and Devlin held his breath. Was she really as restless as he? And why?

Don't get your hopes up, he told himself. The odds were she was just suffering the strain of holding Sam so much today. He could feel the ache himself in every muscle—and he hadn't been the one doing most of the carrying. Kady had.

He rubbed his shoulder and thought wryly that he'd

like to see some of the weight lifters at the gym carry
Sam around for a full day. There was a good deal of
difference between pumping iron and hauling around
twenty pounds of sleeping—or, even worse, unwilling—
kid.

Kady's voice came out of the darkness, as smooth and
light as a spiderweb and, he thought, just as seductively
inviting. "Devlin? Is something wrong?"

"Just some sore muscles. Sorry to disturb you."

"That's okay. I can't seem to sleep, either."

"What's the problem?"

"Oh, my neck hurts a bit. It'll be all right." She hesitated. "You must be uncomfortable down there."

"Yeah." He thought, *And, under the circumstances,
I'd be every bit as restless if I was somewhere else.* But
of course there was no point in telling Kady that he'd
long since given up the idea of sleeping.

He pushed the blankets aside and moved across the
room. She was lying in the precise center of the big bed,
and there was plenty of room on either side of her. If
she'd been any other woman, Devlin might have wondered if she was offering him not only an invitation to
join her, but his choice of positions.

But of course this wasn't just any woman. Kady had
probably chosen that arrangement on purpose, all right,
but not with any intention of enticing him. She'd probably meant to leave the maximum protection zone all the
way around her.

A streak of moonlight fell across the bed and kissed
her hair, and involuntarily his hand went out to touch
the silvery halo.

Kady sat up, graceful despite the speed of her movement. "What are you doing?"

She sounded panicky, and Devlin kept his voice warm
and calm and comforting. "Applying your training," he
said easily, and sat down on the edge of the mattress.

"I was staying close enough to hear in case you woke up and needed reassurance. Now I'm here to pat your back and soothe you to sleep again. Or rub your sore neck, if you'd prefer."

She didn't smile, which surprised him. It wasn't like her not to see the humor in comparing her to Sam.

Instead, she sighed and said, "I can't turn that down."

"Why should you want to? I give great neck rubs." Gently he laid her against the pillows and turned her away from him.

He took his time, using only his fingertips at first till he'd gotten the feel of each muscle. "That's the one that hurts," he said, tracing a line carefully down the side of her neck and across her shoulder.

"How'd you know?"

"Because it's tense. You've got such a tiny little neck—no wonder it's sore from tossing Sam around all day."

He rubbed and kneaded, and slowly she relaxed. He could feel her sinking lower into the mattress—as if her body was sculpted of butter and he'd applied slow heat.

And she wasn't the only one who was feeling the flame, though the fire inside him was a different sort and the result hardly relaxing. At least, he thought philosophically, one of them would get a decent night's rest.

Sam shifted and cried out, and Kady started to sit up. Devlin gently pushed her into the pillows. "Take it easy," he ordered.

He'd have sworn she was half-asleep, and yet automatically she'd responded to the baby's cry almost before Sam had uttered it. The phenomenon was fascinating, Devlin thought. She was a natural mother.

But the baby didn't wake. A moment later he released a tiny snore, and Devlin started gently massaging again.

"Why don't you have kids, Kady?" The question was uttered before it occurred to him that it was not only

intrusive but on the verge of rude. The silence stretched
out as he tried to find a way to apologize.

Her voice was little more than a breath, so soft he had
to strain to hear it. "I want to have more to give my
children than I had."

His hands stilled for a moment and then, very slowly,
he began to rub again. "You have a lot to give them,
Kady."

She didn't answer.

The hypnotic rhythm of the massage began to tell on
Devlin, too. Despite his inner tension, he couldn't fight
off a yawn, and his back was starting to hurt. Sitting on
the edge of the mattress, turned at an angle to best reach
her shoulders, was the most awkward position he'd ever
assumed—short, of course, of that damned rocking chair.

He stopped rubbing for a moment, and Kady murmured something incoherent. A half-conscious protest,
he thought, and smiled. She was too close to sleep for
her self-defense mechanisms to function. This was the
real woman—the real desires—surfacing. And even if
she wanted nothing else from him, at least she liked
having her neck rubbed.

Careful not to jolt the mattress, he stretched out beside
her. If that was what she wanted, he thought, he'd lie
here and massage all night.

The warmth of Devlin's hands on her shoulders soothed
Kady almost to the brink of sleep, but the gentle, knead-
ing pressure of his touch kept her from sliding over the
edge. She let herself drift in that state of half-awareness
where reality blurs and dreams are just a breath away.

You have a lot to give them.

She didn't doubt that Devlin had meant what he'd
said. It was true, after all, and surely it wasn't egotistical
to admit the facts. She'd be a darned good mother—

when the right time came. When she could offer a child a solid home, a secure future, two loving parents…

You have a lot to give them.

A lot to give to kids, he'd meant. Obviously, she didn't have anything to offer that interested him or he wouldn't be so calmly rubbing her neck in the middle of the night. He was so obviously unexcited that he might as well be petting a dog.

She told herself it was only the state of half-sleep in which she floated that made her believe it mattered. Fully awake, she knew, she wouldn't *want* Devlin Cunningham to be attracted to her.

But half-asleep, all she could think of was how fascinated she was with him—and how she wished it was something other than a generous whim to comfort her that had brought him to her bed.

What was so different about her than the women he fancied? Heaven knew there were plenty of them. While she had no doubt that Devlin's taste was discriminating, it was also without question eclectic.

So why not me? she thought rebelliously. What was so wrong with her that she held no attraction for him at all? She might not be gorgeous, but she wasn't exactly hard on the eyes. Her figure wasn't stunning, but she had curves in all the right places. And though he didn't seem to care for her personality, there were plenty of people who liked her immensely.

Oh, he had said once that he admired her legs. That was something, she supposed. And he'd kissed her…once. But after that brief and quickly interrupted caress…nothing.

She wondered what special attraction Sam's mother had held for him. What about her had caught Devlin Cunningham's interest? She'd have been attractive, of course. Probably even charming—she must have been, to hide from him the personality flaw that had allowed her to abandon a helpless child.

Maybe, Kady thought, he'd learned a lesson from that experience. Maybe he was just being careful where she—or any other woman, for that matter—was concerned.

And maybe you're just trying to con yourself, too, whispered a little voice at the back of her brain. Telling herself that it wasn't her fault, that he'd have been attracted to her if not for other factors, was a pretty foolish attempt at consolation.

She didn't know when she passed the boundary into sleep and half-logic gave way to full-fledged dreams. There was so little difference between the two that it was hard to draw the line.

Full sunlight was falling across the bedspread when she roused. Her back was pressed against Devlin's chest, and his arm lay heavy across her waist. His palm cupped the bottom of her rib cage, and his thumb lay against the soft underside of her breast. And his breath stirred her hair and tickled her scalp.

Kady lay very still and tried not to pretend that this was the aftermath of a night of love. While there was nothing overtly sexual about the way he was holding her, it wasn't hard to believe that this was the casual caress of a longtime lover. He seemed as natural as if he'd slept this way on a thousand nights.

But of course, she reminded herself, he probably had. After all, the action doubtless didn't vary much—it was only the woman who changed from time to time.

The thought made her furious, and none too gently she pushed his arm aside and sat up.

Devlin opened his eyes. "Now that's hardly friendly, considering how hard I worked to help you sleep last night."

Obviously, Kady thought, he had no trouble orienting

himself, or remembering that nothing earthshaking had occurred the night before. The thought was unaccountably annoying. "Oh, great," she growled. "I'm glad to know you don't have any trouble rousing up early on some mornings! I suppose as long as there's no work involved—"

Devlin's eyebrows raised a fraction. He punched his pillow into a wad, settling into it with obvious comfort. "Do you always wake up in such a bad temper?"

Kady gritted her teeth. *Only when you're around*, she wanted to say, but she knew better.

From the crib came a throaty giggle. Sam was standing on tiptoe and hanging on tight in order to peek over the rail. Between his clenched hands, his small face bore a smile as brilliant as the sunlight that poured through the front windows.

"Now if that isn't a sight," Devlin muttered. "So much for the idea of a peaceful few minutes before he takes over the day."

Kady slid out of bed and went to the child. "It's just as well. If you'd had a peaceful few minutes, you'd only have gone back to sleep."

"Or kissed you," he said casually. "In an attempt to improve your mood, of course. Though I expect instead of doing any good, it would have really messed things up."

Kady, already bending over the crib with Sam's arms tightening trustingly around her neck, jumped in surprise.

"Are you all right?" Devlin asked. He was standing uncomfortably close behind her.

He's not touching you, Kady told herself. *You cannot possibly feel the heat of his body. It's your imagination.* "My neck twinged again when Sam grabbed hold." It was a lie, but Devlin would have no reason to suspect that. She couldn't let him see how much his careless comment had shaken her.

And it was no more than a careless comment, she was certain. For one thing, he couldn't have thought it through or he wouldn't have said anything so irritating. Devlin Cunningham was far too smooth an operator to make a slip like that.

In fact, Kady told herself, she ought to be thoroughly offended. So he believed that kissing her would mess things up, did he? No doubt he was afraid Kady would jump to conclusions about his intentions. How incredibly egotistical of him to assume such a thing! Much as she'd like to take him seriously, she was smarter than that.

Listen to yourself, she ordered. *Wanting to take him seriously? You're slowly losing your mind, Kady Bishop.*

"Da-da," Sam said happily, and put his head down on Kady's shoulder.

"See?" she said automatically. "I told you that didn't mean anything. Now he's calling *me* da-da."

"I guess you're right. That means you win the prize and get to cook his breakfast," Devlin murmured. "Aren't you the lucky one?"

She smiled sweetly. "Of course I am. While I'm fixing his cereal, you can change his diaper."

The look on Devlin's face almost made her feel cheerful again.

Kady was dishing up cereal and yogurt when Devlin came into the kitchen with Sam in one arm. The baby was still in his pajamas, but Devlin had put on fresh jeans and a crisp pin-striped shirt with the sleeves rolled above the elbow.

Casual as it was, the combination made Kady, who was once again wrapped in his brocade smoking jacket, feel severely underdressed. Not that Devlin called any attention to her attire—but it wasn't much comfort to realize that he probably wouldn't have paid any attention even if she'd been wearing nothing at all.

She took a deep breath. "I made coffee. And I'm toasting the rolls that were left over from last night, if you want some."

"That sounds good." Devlin waved a sheet of paper at her. "My grandmother has been burning up the fax lines again." He reached for two mugs from the cabinet shelf.

"Really? Where is she by now?" Kady set Sam's cereal in front of him and tied a bib around his neck. He banged his spoon into the dish, splattering rice across the table.

"Apparently, she's in the Canary Islands."

"Well, at least she's back in civilization." Kady frowned. "I wonder what she's doing there."

Devlin flicked a fingertip against the fax. "Judging by this, she's worrying about whether I'll remember the picnic."

"I can't think why she'd be concerned about *that*," Kady murmured. "How could you possibly forget an event you're so enthusiastic about attending?" The oven timer buzzed, and she pulled a pan from under the broiler.

Devlin eyed the neat, thin-cut slices of cinnamon toast. "Did you need a knife to slice those," he asked genially, "or did you just use the sharp edge of your tongue?"

"If you're going to be like that, I won't share."

"Too late. You already offered—and what kind of example would it make for Sam if you reneged on the deal now?" He snagged a hot slice from the pan and bit into it. "That's good."

"You sound surprised," Kady said crisply.

"I didn't mean it that way. It's just that I'd never have

thought of doing this with a bunch of leftover rolls—I'd have tossed them out.''

"And gone hungry? Waste not, want not." Kady picked up a piece of toast, holding it carefully by the edges so it wouldn't burn her fingers. "Iris didn't mention the time of her flight into O'Hare on Tuesday, by any chance?''

"Why would she? I'm not the one who's supposed to meet her.''

Kady shrugged. "I thought she might have asked you to pass the word along, since she knows I'll be at the picnic, too. Though, on second thought, if she didn't trust you to get there without a reminder..."

"Keep it up," Devlin threatened, "and for Christmas I'll get you a miniature Swiss Army knife with the blades welded shut.''

As if he'd even remember this conversation by the time Christmas came around! "I beg your pardon," Kady said sweetly. "I'll certainly try to be more respectful of your little foibles in the future.''

"And pigs will grow wings, too," Devlin muttered. "What's the deal with the flight times, anyway? Don't you already know which plane she'll be on?''

"Of course not. When she left, she wasn't even sure which month she'd be home, much less which flight." Kady scooped a lump of cereal off Sam's bib and expertly inserted it in his mouth. "That means there's probably a fax from her on my machine, too. Which reminds me—I got my phone messages yesterday, but I can't pick up my faxes without actually stopping at my apartment.''

"And since you still don't have shoes, we'll need to make a side trip on the way to the orphanage.''

"I keep telling you—"

"It's not an orphanage. I know." Devlin frowned thoughtfully at the fax and reached for another slice of cinnamon toast. "That was an interesting question you had. Why *is* she in the Canary Islands? Does she have friends there?"

"None that I've heard of. But maybe they're new friends, people she met on her trip. Or maybe she knows someone who's vacationing there and she's changed her plans and decided to join them for a few days. There's nothing she has to come home for just now, is there?"

"Why would you expect me to know? The last time Iris filled me in on her schedule, I was about twelve years old."

"Or maybe she does it regularly but you just don't listen."

"Possible," Devlin conceded.

"Maybe she'll stay a while, and give you a chance to get this all sorted out." She glanced at the baby.

As if he knew he was being discussed, Sam chuckled and splashed his cereal again.

Devlin looked doubtful. "How long do you think she's likely to stay away? Even if I could hide the kid, clearing the baby things out of the town house will take a week."

"I'm certainly not suggesting you strangle Sam and bury him in the nearest flower bed! I just meant it might be nice to have a little more time to figure out what to tell Iris, that's all."

"Now you're finally getting helpful." Devlin leaned against the counter and folded his arms across his chest. "What do you suggest I do?"

"Tell the truth, of course. But there are ways to—I don't mean to slant the facts, exactly, but to interpret them in a way that will lessen the damage."

Devlin looked doubtful.

"For instance, if you straightforwardly admit your responsibility, your grandmother will have to respect you for being honest, even though she isn't going to like the facts. But if you keep trying to deny that Sam is yours—''

"I'll keep that in mind," Devlin murmured.

"And he's such a darling baby, I don't see how Iris could help falling in love with him." Her eyes widened. "That's the way to do it, Devlin! You meet her at the airport on Tuesday with Sam in tow. She won't even have time to be angry, because the moment she sees him—''

"Now that, Kady my dear," he mused, "is the idea of a lifetime."

Kady's heart lifted. She was certain that the reluctance to face Iris—understandable though it was—was the largest stumbling block remaining to threaten Devlin's wholehearted acceptance of his son. But once he had faced his grandmother squarely and openly... "You can present her with a fait accompli," she said.

"In a manner of speaking," Devlin murmured. "And you'll go along, of course."

"Me? Why would you want me?"

"You can be the buffer zone. In fact, you could even be the one to point out how cute Sam is—stunning evidence of the quality of the Cunningham gene pool. That should make her feel really proud."

"Devlin, I'm not so sure that's a good idea."

"Well, we'll work out the details later. We've got a couple of days, after all." He glanced at the baby. "And, with any luck, it won't take more than forty-eight hours to chisel the cereal off Sam's face so Iris can get a decent look at him."

Sam crowed with laughter and banged his spoon.

Kady sighed. "Are you done, Sam?"

"No," the baby said.

She glanced at the kitchen clock. "Nevertheless, if we're going to be on time for the picnic..."

"Must we?" Devlin asked hopefully. "We could always plead that we couldn't get away because we were being held hostage."

"By a year-old terrorist armed only with a dish of rice cereal?"

"We don't have to go into the details," Devlin argued.

Kady ignored him. "Do you have a washer and dryer?"

"In the closet under the stairs. Why?"

"I'm going to gather up a load of laundry so we don't have to keep buying new clothes for Sam." She plucked the baby out of his chair, skimmed the cereal-coated sleeper off him and handed him to Devlin. "You're in charge of bath time. Make sure the water isn't too hot, and don't move from beside him—he can climb out of the sink, and he doesn't have enough sense not to."

She didn't know which of them looked more dismayed, but the identical looks of distrust were almost enough to make her laugh. "And be careful with the shampoo, okay? Too much and you'll be rinsing for a week."

"Now that," Devlin said grimly, "sounds promising."

Kady took her time with the laundry, spot-treating each of Sam's tiny garments. How could a child who was so small get into so many different messes?

Even over the rumble of the washing machine she could hear Sam's voluble protests. *He has to learn*, she told herself, and then started to wonder which of the two males she meant.

She heard only a couple of muffled comments from Devlin and suspected that they were barely fit to print. It would serve him right, she thought, if Sam chose Tuesday to start talking and Devlin as a role model.

On the other hand, Kady decided, since she didn't want to be around to see Iris Cunningham's reaction to a great grandson who swore like a pipe fitter, perhaps she'd better intervene before the situation got completely out of hand.

The kitchen looked as if it had been bombarded with water balloons. Soap dripped from Sam's curls, from his eyelashes, from the end of his nose. Devlin wasn't in much better shape—there was a clump of shampoo suds perched atop his left ear, and he'd been splattered from head to foot. The front of his shirt was so wet it clung to his chest.

"Why do we build bridges out of concrete," he asked almost breathlessly, "when rice cereal is so much harder and more durable?"

"Give me that shirt," Kady ordered. "I'll throw it in the washer right now."

"It doesn't need to be washed. Sam's already taken care of that part." But Devlin unbuttoned the shirt and peeled it away from his wet skin.

Kady had seen his chest—heaven knew he wandered around the town house often enough in half-buttoned shirts that did little to conceal the breadth of his shoulders. But she had to admit she'd never gotten the full effect before.

He paused with one arm still in a sleeve to scoop the coffeepot out of Sam's reach.

Kady hadn't realized, for instance, how quickly and gracefully he could move. The muscles in his arms and shoulders seemed to ripple without the slightest effort.

"Do you want the jeans, too?" Devlin asked. "They're just as wet." His hand hovered over the snap where the soft gold hair that covered his chest tapered down to a slim arrow and vanished under the waistband of his jeans.

"No," she said, and hastily added, as he started to smile, "that's a different load altogether."

"No doubt," Devlin murmured.

Sam grinned at Kady, seized two tiny handfuls of Devlin's chest hair and hauled himself up till he was standing in the sink.

Devlin winced. "Sam, that's not a grab rail!"

"It worked, didn't it?" Kady murmured.

Devlin picked up a washcloth and flung it across the kitchen at her. Kady didn't dodge quite in time, and the dripping cloth glanced across her cheek. "Good shot," she complimented as she picked it up and headed to the washer to put in Devlin's shirt.

At least he'd forgotten about the jeans.

KADY'S apartment, one of the smallest units in the complex, smelled hot and stale from being closed up over the long weekend. But her eagerness to escape the cloying atmosphere wasn't the only reason she hurried as she packed an overnight bag. She'd left Devlin and Sam making faces at each other in the parking lot, but she didn't want to test the patience level of either one of them. Besides, the picnic was due to start in half an hour, and the drive across town to Oakwood School would take at least half that time.

She shoved her feet into the first pair of sandals she found and was still tossing essentials into her bag when the doorbell rang. "I'm hurrying," she muttered, and went to fling the door open. "Darn it, if you can't handle a baby on your own for two lousy minutes, how do you expect to—"

The figure in the doorway wasn't Devlin, however, but the male half of the young couple who lived in Seven B, just down the hall.

"Oh," Kady said inadequately. "Sorry, Jeff. I thought you were someone else. I have to go out again in a minute, but what can I do for you in the meantime?"

"Liz sent me down to check on you. She's been worried all weekend because your car was here and you weren't—and it's so unlike you to go away and not tell anyone."

Kady's heart melted. "Thanks, Jeff. It's sweet of you both to be concerned. Things happened sort of suddenly, and I didn't even think to let you know that I was staying with a friend."

Jeff nodded sagely. "Must have been an exciting weekend, to make you forget."

"Well, no, it wasn't all that exci—" She stopped in mid-word as the sound of footsteps echoed round the corner from the main hall. Even before Devlin came into sight, Kady knew it was him.

When, she wondered, had she started listening so closely to his movements that she could identify his foot-steps?

Sam crowed with delight when he saw Kady and stretched out both arms to her.

"I hate to rush you," Devlin said, "but the baby was beginning to miss you."

Jeff grinned. "Well, well," he murmured. "I'd like to see what you'd call exciting, Kady, if this isn't it." With a casual wave, he vanished down the hall.

Kady pushed the door wide. "At least come on in so the rest of the tenants don't get a free floor show."

"All I said was—"

"Never mind. I'm almost ready."

Devlin stood in the middle of her tiny living room, looking around, while she returned to her bedroom to finish packing. "I know it's a scary thought, but maybe we have more in common than I realized," he said when she returned carrying her bag. "This even looks like my place—a desk in the living room, files stacked on the dining room table..."

Kady shook her head. "Not even close. I don't own a single comic book."

"You have no idea what you're missing. Was that the man you were talking to on the phone yesterday?"

"When I picked up my messages, you mean, and you were listening in? Is that why you went out of your way to discourage him?"

"But I didn't," Devlin said earnestly. "If I ever do, you'll know it."

Kady gritted her teeth. Fool, she told herself, to imagine for even an instant that Devlin Cunningham might give more than casual attention to any man she knew!

Devlin reached for her bag, and Kady pulled the door open and snapped the spring lock.

"No fax from Iris, after all?" he asked.

Kady was not only startled, but annoyed with herself—the fax machine was one of the main reasons they'd made this side trip in the first place. "I forgot to check," she admitted.

To his credit, Devlin didn't say a word. But the way he looked at her, Kady thought, spoke volumes.

The fax machine was on her desk, in the corner of the living room. Unlike the big, expensive model Devlin had installed in the town house, Kady's was the economy version, with no fancy lights or bells to tell her whether there'd been activity since she'd last checked. She ran a hand over the back of the machine and pulled up a long strip of paper.

One of the messages was from Iris, of course, just as she'd expected. She tore the paper off the machine and glanced over the neatly written paragraphs. "Oh, that's cute. She wants me to phone you to be sure you're up in time for the picnic—" She gasped.

"What's wrong?"

She stared at him, wide-eyed. "Iris won't be home on Tuesday, after all."

"Well, that's good news, surely. You said yourself I could benefit from a little extra time."

Kady shook her head. "You don't have two days to get ready to face her. You've only got one." She held the fax out to him. "She's coming home *tomorrow*."

CHAPTER EIGHT

DEVLIN gave a long, thoughtful whistle. "I guess that shoots your idea of Iris vacationing with friends in the Canary Islands for a week or two, doesn't it?"

Kady was astounded. "Aren't you even upset?"

"Any particular reason I should be?"

"Well, she's apt to want a few details, like when Sam was born and who his mother is. And since you still don't seem to have the vaguest idea where he came from—"

Devlin shrugged. "Judging from the trouble I've had so far, an extra twenty-four hours isn't likely to tell me anything more. So what difference does it make which day Iris comes home?" He parked Sam in his car seat once more and eyed Kady with interest as he started the engine. "The real question, I'd say, is why you're wound so tight about it."

And an excellent question it was, Kady told herself. Why should it be so important to her that Devlin handle this well? But of course, it was Sam she was concerned about. That poor little guy needed all the goodwill he could get, from any source. If Iris took an interest in him, it might at least help make up for the lack of a mother in his life. But if Devlin's careless approach turned his grandmother off...

"It certainly wouldn't be any of my business how you handle your domestic troubles," she said tartly, "if it wasn't for how it's likely to affect Sam. And then, of course, there's the minor fact that you insist on dragging me into your affairs. I don't happen to like scenes, and this is apt to be a dandy.''

"Do you think so?" Devlin murmured. "I suppose you're right. By the way, why don't you like scenes? I'd have thought, since this one was your idea—"

"*My* idea? What are you talking about?"

"Your suggestion that I take Sam to the airport. I can't wait to see my grandmother's face when I walk up to her on the concourse and say, 'Hi, Iris, this is Sam—and if you're wondering how I ended up with a baby, your guess is probably as good as mine.'''

Kady shuddered. "This is no time for flippancy, and you'd already know that if you had the intelligence of—of…''

"A dustpan?" Devlin said helpfully. He started to whistle cheerfully and broke off to add, "In fact, I'm looking forward to this encounter with Iris. The sooner, the better… What would I do without you, Kady?"

Kady told herself there was no point in talking to him. The man had clearly lost all touch with reality. But she couldn't put the problem out of her mind, either. For Sam's sake, she had to at least try to convince Devlin how important it was that he handle this properly.

Her fingertips drummed against the leather armrest with the same dull rhythm as the questions that circled in her brain, and with the same lack of result.

"I've got it," Devlin said. "I'll just tell Iris *you're* his mom."

Kady turned her head so fast her sore neck muscles snapped like rubber bands. "Ouch!" She put a hand to the side of her neck, but the pain was minor compared to the shock of his words. "What in the hell do you mean? In the first place, Iris wouldn't believe you for a moment. I didn't even know you two years ago, so how could I—"

"Want me to rub your neck again?"

"I want you to stop making stupid statements! How could I possibly be Sam's mother? Unless you're thinking of trying to get out of your responsibility by foisting the entire thing onto me. And if that's the case, I warn you, Cunningham, I won't—"

"I meant, of course, his *new* mom."

Kady choked. She felt as if she'd swallowed her tongue.

"But we can talk about all that later," Devlin added calmly. "Here we are at Oakwood—and it looks as if events are about to get under way."

He was right about that, Kady noted with dismay. The resident students, all dressed in navy-blue uniforms, had lined up in neat rows on the front lawn of the Victorian mansion that housed the school, and a group of dignitaries had already gathered on the front porch, where the public address system was in place. And all of them appeared to be watching the gate.

It was possible that somewhere on the grounds there was a pair of eyes that wasn't focused on Devlin's sleek black sports car, but Kady wouldn't have cared to bet on it.

Across the lawn toward them marched a gray-haired matron. She caught Devlin's eye and pointed toward a small plot of grass, and he maneuvered the car onto it.

Kady cleared her throat, though her voice sounded as rough as if it had been bottled up for a year. "Nice of the headmistress to save a parking spot for you. Of course, Iris probably faxed her, too, to let her know that you were bound to be running late."

Devlin shook his head sadly. "I did warn you about that tongue of yours, Bishop."

Kady was barely listening. "Oh, great. Here comes the entire board of directors."

She fixed a smile on her face and slid out of the car.

The headmistress looked from Kady to Devlin and back, and blinked. "I was becoming concerned about you, Kady," she said. "You're always right on time."

"And Devlin never is," Kady agreed. "Miss Anderson, you've met Mrs. Cunningham's grandson, of course?"

Devlin flashed a smile of quite devastating charm. Kady was annoyed to see that the headmistress fell for it.

"Of course," Miss Anderson said. "It was some time ago, however. And I never expected that the two of you..."

Kady said quickly, "Iris asked me to make sure he got here."

The tallest and sternest member of the board of directors had stooped to stare in the car window. "And who's *this*?"

Devlin said, calmly, "Oh, that's Sam."

Kady had to admire his presence of mind. She would have been scrambling for an explanation. Devlin, on the other hand, had very precisely answered the only question that had been asked and ignored the unspoken ones. Still, she thought, what on earth was keeping him from admitting the facts? Surely he wasn't still doubtful. If he'd only admit that the baby was his...

Devlin unfastened the safety buckle on Sam's seat and lifted him out. The moment he was out of the car, Sam reached for Kady. She took him from Devlin's arms, and the baby yawned hugely, murmured something which could—to a suspicious ear—sound like *mama*, and put his head down on her shoulder.

Devlin smiled and patted Kady on the back. "Doesn't it make you feel all warm and cuddly to know that's the most secure spot in his entire little universe?"

Kady gritted her teeth. What was it he'd said about a

warning? What a fiendishly effective way to exact revenge!

The director looked coldly at her. "I had no idea how long it had been since I'd seen you, Kady. In fact, I didn't even know you were married."

Devlin looked puzzled. "Oh, she's not."

"Thanks a bunch, Cunningham," Kady muttered. "As a matter of fact, I don't have a baby, either."

"Not just yet," Devlin agreed. "But only because we're still discussing the matter. However, we really don't have time to pursue it just now, do we?" He slipped a hand under the headmistress's elbow and turned her toward the porch steps. "Isn't it time for the ceremonies to start?"

The board of directors followed dutifully behind, and as soon as they were out of hearing range, Kady looked at Sam. "Do you have any idea how badly your mother—whoever she is—has messed up my reputation? And as for your father..."

Sam looked a little worried.

Kady cuddled him closer. "No, it's not your fault," she soothed. "But next time he picks you up, why don't you bite him? He deserves it."

Devlin was testing the microphone, and Kady moved away from the crowd. She didn't want to listen. The reverberations of the public address system reminded her of the way his words had echoed through her head a few minutes ago, setting off an earthquake of emotion.

His new mom...

How very much, she admitted, she would like to be Sam's mother.

Of course, it was hardly the sort of romantic proposal any woman dreamed of. If, indeed, he'd meant it to be a proposal at all. It was hard to tell what Devlin had in mind. Kady supposed he might have been referring to some wacky kind of foster-care arrangement, and not marriage at all.

Marriage.

Surely he couldn't have meant any such thing.

But the very word, once she had admitted it to her conscious mind, seemed to take on a life of its own. It was like baby shampoo, she thought helplessly, bubbling up with only the slightest encouragement into mounds of suds, irrepressible and unmanageable. The vision of herself married to Devlin Cunningham was every bit as untamable.

Pictures danced through her mind, half memory, half imagination. She could actually see, as if she were floating above his big bed, the two of them snuggling there, not as they had this morning but with the easy intimacy of lovers. She could picture them together in the black marble bathtub. She could close her eyes and see Sam running through a park, his small hands linked with theirs. Images flashed past with lightning speed, images of them together, laughing, learning…loving.

Unable to flee any longer, Kady squared her shoulders and faced the truths that had been nagging at her since yesterday. Yes, she would like very much to be Sam's mother. She had tumbled head over heels for that small boy.

But she had fallen far harder for his father. The idea of being Sam's mother was a joy, but being Devlin's wife would be a dream come true.

The really scary part of that admission was the undeniable knowledge that her attraction to him was not new. Her sudden love affair with Sam had not precipitated her feelings for Devlin, only brought them abruptly and painfully into sharp focus.

Kady had been fascinated by Devlin Cunningham since their first meeting. She'd always known that, though she'd told herself the reasons were unpleasant ones. And though she didn't know when fascination had metamorphosed into love, it didn't really matter, she supposed, precisely when it had happened. The fact was that it had.

She was as stunningly lost in love as it was possible for a woman to be.

At least now she knew why she'd been so annoyed at Shelle Emerson's head tosses and coy laughter and so irritated by the casual way Devlin had treated Shelle and the other women in his life. Kady had wanted all his attention for herself.

But she had never come close to getting it, she reminded herself, even throughout this weekend with its forced intimacy—for there was Sam.

And Sam was the only reason Devlin was interested in her now. He certainly would never have hinted at marriage—if, she reminded herself yet again, marriage was what he'd meant at all—had he not found himself with a year-old kid on his hands. A kid who needed a caregiver…or maybe even a mother.

That realization hurt the most of all—knowing that Devlin didn't want a wife, that he would never have considered making her any sort of proposal if it hadn't been for Sam.

She looked at the baby, who'd fallen asleep in her arms. It wasn't Sam's fault. He was the innocent bystander in all this.

How, she thought in sudden fury, could Devlin have been so oblivious to his own conduct as not even to suspect the existence of a pregnancy? What kind of a man, presented with his child, wouldn't even have an idea about who that baby's mother was? What sort of human being could offer the position to another woman as blithely as if he was offering a choice of chocolate or vanilla?

Maybe, Kady thought, she should be pleased he

hadn't put that offer of his on any sort of personal terms! The man was incapable of loving, incapable of establishing any sort of lasting relationship—except, perhaps, on the kind of businesslike terms he'd seemed to be suggesting. At least he'd been honest enough not to pretend to have fallen in love with her....

What was she thinking? Kady asked herself in horror. Being Sam's mother would be one thing. Being Devlin's wife—on any sort of terms—would be a recipe for madness.

And she'd better not forget it.

The keynote speaker droned on. Devlin wondered if someone had neglected to tell him that his primary audience wasn't a convention of political hacks but a group of kids far more interested in lunch and games.

It was amazing, he thought as his gaze drifted over the long rows of navy-blue uniforms, that there was no more than a hint of restlessness in the ranks. No doubt that was because the headmistress, beside him on the platform, was watching her charges intently. He wondered if she was hearing any more of the speech than the kids were.

He half-closed his eyes and pictured Kady standing in the midst of the group, as she would have looked at least five years ago. Navy would have been exactly the wrong color for her, he thought, though he suspected that even as a teenager she would have overcome the drab garments and made them appear to have some style. Surely she hadn't acquired that grace of movement overnight, along with her university degree. She must have showed signs of it even as a child. Perhaps that was what had made her stand out from the crowd—as she must have done, to have drawn Iris's attention.

What would she have been thinking as she stood straight and square-shouldered in that line of students?

Would she have been listening to the speech or thinking of her plans for the future or keeping an eye on the younger children?

Maybe all three, he thought. The super-efficient Miss Bishop could have managed to pull it off. Funny, though, that the trait that had annoyed him most about her in the beginning was now one that intrigued him.

He shifted slightly in his chair and let his gaze wander farther afield. A spot of fuchsia caught his eye, out near the gate at the end of the drive. Her head was bent over Sam, her dark hair almost concealing the baby's bright curls. There was something incredibly soft about her where that child was concerned, unlike the prickles she displayed around Devlin.

Of course, that was quite a kid. He couldn't deny feeling drawn to Sam himself. Yes, he thought, it ought to be very interesting to see his grandmother's reaction tomorrow when she met Sam. In fact, he was half-tempted to carry out that idle threat and tell Iris that Kady was the baby's mother, just to see what they'd both do. Kady had practically choked to death on the suggestion the first time around—but had that been simple surprise or actual horror?

The speaker droned to a halt, to be greeted by half-hearted applause. Devlin sprang to his feet before the speaker could take the clapping as encouragement to start in again, and announced that the games would begin as soon as possible.

The students cheered and broke ranks, streaming across the lawn toward the side of the mansion. The headmistress fixed him with a glare. "I hadn't intended to release them just yet," she said.

"I'm so sorry," Devlin murmured, without an ounce of repentance. "Shall I try to round them all up for you again?"

She sniffed and turned to the speaker with a gracious

smile. Devlin leaned against the rail and looked for Kady.

She'd moved away from the gate, and it was a full minute before he spotted her not far from the mansion, in the midst of a group of girls of all ages, the one bright spot of fuchsia in a navy sea.

He had no trouble remembering how heavy Sam could be, relaxed in sleep. The weight must be dragging at the sore muscles in her neck, in her shoulders. He started down the driveway, at a deceptively lazy pace, to meet her.

The group of girls split to let him reach Kady's side.

"See?" he said gently. "You should have swapped jobs with me when I offered—you'd be all done by now."

"Somehow I doubt you'll be asked to be master of ceremonies again."

"Oh? Why?"

"Because usually after the main speaker finishes, the headmistress says a few words, and the chairman of the board of directors thanks everyone for coming, and two or three of the main patrons make a few remarks—"

"My mistake," Devlin said sweetly. "That's what comes from lack of experience."

Kady let him take Sam without even a hint of protest. Obviously he'd been right about her muscles, because she rubbed her shoulder. "Besides, you've got the hard job, now. All I have to do is play games. I was looking for a place to put him down, but—"

"I'll try to stand up to the challenge."

One of the patrons came up to them, beaming. "You must be Iris's grandson," she said, bubbling, and patted Devlin's arm. "What a beautiful baby! Is he yours?"

Devlin looked at Sam as if he'd never seen the child before. He heard Kady draw in a deep, apprehensive breath, and pure mischief made him prolong the moment. "It certainly *appears* that way," he murmured.

The patron stroked Sam's cheek. "How old is he?"

Devlin smiled blindingly and confided, "I don't have a clue."

A couple of the girls giggled. Kady closed her eyes and appeared to be in pain. The patron looked down her nose and stalked off.

Kady shooed the girls away to set up the first games and turned on Devlin as soon as they were gone. "Now that's a fine lesson to be giving them!"

He opened his eyes very wide. "Would you have preferred that I lie?"

She growled a little.

It was, Devlin thought, a very sensual sound. He told himself not to dwell on it. "I came down here to say nice things to you, and you try to get me to commit perjury."

"What kind of things?"

She couldn't keep herself from asking, Devlin thought, and a smile quirked the corner of his mouth. "So the lady's interested after all?"

"Never mind." She spun away.

He caught up with her in two strides and dropped into step beside her. "Just that I'd noticed how popular you seem to be. But of course it's natural for the students to look up to you and want to follow in your footsteps."

She paused. "Do you think so?"

She sounded breathless, surprised—almost doubtful. Devlin was startled. Did she think he was making it up just to win favor? Or was she really so modest that she had no idea of the effect she could have on these girls?

Whichever it was, there wasn't time to pursue the question with a hundred young people waiting impatiently for the first race to begin. And it wouldn't be a good idea to drop a careless kiss on the tip of her nose, either, no matter how that upturned face was pleading to be caressed. Kady would deny she was asking for it— for she couldn't see the softness in her face, the sheen of interest in her eyes.

Of course, he reminded himself, if he dared to kiss her, she probably wouldn't settle for a mere denial—not with this audience. She'd no doubt sock him in the solar plexus for good measure.

"We'll talk about it later," he said.

He dropped down beside an age-old walnut tree where he could see every move she made and arranged Sam in his lap.

Kady took the whistle one of the girls offered and stepped up on a nearby tree stump to summon the students to gather around her. They formed a large, rough circle around her, attentive and respectful. He felt a momentary fancy that they were looking to her not only for the rules of the game but for life itself. It would be natural enough. He was sure the headmistress didn't let an opportunity slip to remind her charges that Kady was one of Oakwood's successes, a beacon for their futures.

He looked at Sam, snoring peacefully. What about his future? His—and Sam's?

Did Kady Bishop fit into that puzzle? And—if so— where?

The picnic was over, the last of the food demolished, the modest fireworks exploded, before Kady had a chance for another private word with Devlin. The baby was yawning in the back of the car as they drove across Chicago toward Devlin's town house, and the silence was uncomfortably thick.

Was Devlin simply bored, Kady wondered, by what must have been—for an outsider—an incredibly dull day? Was he regretting the half offer he'd made, or con-

cerned that she might take it the wrong way and assume
a proposal that hadn't actually been voiced?

"About that suggestion you made," she began
abruptly.

At the same instant, Devlin said, "I'm awfully
sorry—"

They both stopped awkwardly. "Go on," Kady said.

"You first. Which suggestion?"

That, she thought irritably, certainly answered one
question—the issue might be of burning importance to
her, but if he didn't even remember…! "That I be Sam's
new mother."

In the dusk, she sensed rather than saw the quirk of
his eyebrows. "And now that you've thought about it?"

"*Nyet* interested. I have enough to do without taking
on a foster child." Kady found herself holding her breath
as she waited for his answer, and was thoroughly annoyed. What was the matter with her, anyway? Why did
she even care what he said? She certainly didn't expect
him to explain that she'd misunderstood—that he'd been
asking her to be his wife. If that was the case he
wouldn't have had to be reminded.

In any event, she'd already decided that even if he
had meant marriage, she'd turn him down flat. So why
was she anxious about his answer?

Devlin said carelessly, "Well, I just thought Iris
would be happier that way. You're so eminently respect-
able, you see."

At least she hadn't made a fool of herself by jumping
to unwarranted conclusions. And she was glad not to
have to extricate herself from an unwanted proposal.

You're relieved, Kady told herself. *And don't forget
it.*

Another day or two and her promise, so rashly given,
would be fulfilled. She would have done what she could

to ease Sam's adjustment, and she'd be free to take up
her life where Devlin had interrupted it.

Interrupted? What a bland, monotonous impression
that gave to an episode that had been neither! Devlin
hadn't merely interrupted her life, he'd blasted it into
fragments. Kady would be lucky if she could ever fit the
bits back together into a reasonable whole—for now that
she knew she loved him, she was terrified there would
always be a great chunk missing.

She set her jaw with determination. She would do as
she had always done. She would go on, regardless.

Traffic was light and moving fast, and as the sports
car flashed down the street in front of the town house
and turned the corner toward the garage entrance, Kady
almost missed the woman standing across the street, apparently watching the front door.

Kady craned her neck to look back, and the image
was seared in her memory. The woman stood on the
sidewalk, her hands in the pockets of her jeans. Her hair
was very pale. In fact, the streetlights made it look almost silver. But she was young. No more than thirty,
Kady thought, and tall and slim.

"Did you see that woman?" she asked.

Devlin punched the button that opened the garage
door. "The one waiting to cross the street? What about
her?"

"I thought she was watching the house."

"How could you tell what she was watching, with
those dark glasses she was wearing?"

"Don't you think that's odd? The sunglasses, I mean.
It's past sunset."

Devlin shrugged. "There are any number of reasons
besides strong light to wear dark glasses."

Kady wanted to ask, *Is she Sam's mother*? It was a
stupid question, of course. What reason was there to suspect she was? There were a million tall, slim, very blond

women, and a number of them no doubt had good reason to cross this street. Just because Kady couldn't have walked away from a child without a backward glance didn't mean that Sam's mother would feel the urge to check on him.

As soon as they were inside, Kady slipped to the front windows and looked out. The woman was gone.

She told herself it wasn't really relief she felt, for it would have been good for all of them to know the truth about Sam's mother, to have the mystery over. No, of course she wasn't relieved that the woman had turned out to be only a passerby. She'd simply been worried about being watched.

Though of course she was concerned for Sam. It wasn't the mystery of who the baby's mother was that bothered Kady so much as it was the unknown woman's intentions—if, indeed, she had any where her son was concerned. Abandoning him was bad enough, but if she was to drift in and out of his life...

Baby giggles interrupted Kady's musing, and she turned from the window to see Devlin stretched on the floor, his feet under a desk, with Sam sitting astride his chest, bouncing. It was so obvious both were having fun that Kady smiled involuntarily.

Something had changed today, or perhaps last night, when Devlin and Sam had fallen asleep together. Devlin was softer somehow, gentler, more open to the child. More relaxed, Kady thought, as if he'd finally accepted the fact that his life was forever changed. And almost cheerful, as if he'd come to relish the idea. He still hadn't actually admitted that Sam was his son, but surely, she told herself, that wasn't far off, either.

Devlin swung Sam into the air, and the baby shrieked with delight. Both of them seemed oblivious to her, and though Kady knew she should be happy because the

scene showed such promise for their future, her heart
felt as if it had been wrenched loose from its moorings.

They were such an attractive pair—the handsome
man, so tall, so strong and so gentle even as he rough-
housed with the child. The baby, so transparently ex-
cited, so trusting.

If only, she thought, *they could both be mine.*

Kady forced herself back to reality. She was crazy to
consider anything of the sort, even for a few moments,
and she knew it. But perhaps it was just as well that
unknown woman outside the town house had appeared,
to refresh her memory—for it would be so easy to forget,
to think about acting on the love she felt.

Loving Devlin was one thing. It was foolish, perhaps,
but it was understandable. Mingling her life with his,
however, would be something else. A man who couldn't
even name the mother of his child was just about the
farthest thing Kady could imagine from an advertisement
for lifelong commitment. And as for a man who couldn't
count all the potential mothers on the fingers of both
hands—well, that sort of Don Juan didn't even bear
thinking of.

She wanted more than that.

There had not been a lot of men in her life, and never
one who had tempted her to commitment—for the only
things she had been truly serious about were her education and later her business. There would be time eventually for the other things. Once she'd laid the founda-
tions for a good life, she'd take her time and look around
and choose.

Well, she'd chosen, all right.

Though it was only fair to note in her defense that
she hadn't really had any choice about falling in love
with Devlin. She'd been taken unawares, completely off
guard. She'd thought she wasn't ready for love—and so
love had sneaked past her while her guard was down.

It was no wonder she'd seen Devlin as desirable. She wasn't blind, after all, and her instincts were in normal working condition. It was no more surprising that she found him attractive than that the other hundred women in his life did.

But even as she told herself that glib story, she was uneasily aware it was not quite the truth. What she felt for him was so much more than attraction, so much more than desire, so much more than mere feminine instinct. How could she explain the chemistry of love?

But love, despite the proverb, couldn't conquer everything. It couldn't make all things come out right in the end.

Devlin was excitement, no doubt about that. But Kady wanted stability. She wanted her children to have one father, one man who would be a steady, solid presence for all their lives.

Devlin was fascination, but she wanted trust. She didn't want to worry each time he was out of her sight that another, more attractive woman might catch his eye.

He was tumult, and Kady needed serenity. If there could be one Sam in Devlin Cunningham's life, what was to say there couldn't be another?

That was why, even if that silly suggestion of his *had* been a marriage proposal, she'd have turned him down without a second thought.

At least, she'd like to think that was what she would have done.

CHAPTER NINE

SAM was hungry again, and by the time he'd polished off the prime rib left from last night's dinner, it was getting late. Kady handed him over to Devlin and said, "You clean up the baby and I'll deal with the kitchen."

Devlin looked as if he'd like to argue, and Sam was positively mutinous, yelling and leaning dangerously out of Devlin's arms to reach for Kady.

"It's only a guess," Devlin murmured, "but I think perhaps he'd rather have you."

"Too bad," Kady said. "Things are tough all over, Sam, and I need some time to myself." She felt a little hard-hearted, but it was true enough—the picnic had been exhausting, in more ways than one. And since, in a couple of days, Sam wouldn't have her to reach for at all, he might as well get used to relying on Devlin.

A couple of days. Or maybe even less, if she could come up with a logical reason to break her promise—a reason that couldn't possibly arouse Devlin's suspicions. How thrilled she'd be if she could call a cab right now and go home tonight!

Or would she? Had her promise to stay through the weekend turned into a very convenient excuse?

If Devlin were to say to her right now, *Thanks for the help but we're doing fine, so go on with your life…*

She wouldn't feel relief, Kady admitted. She'd be disappointed, upset at having to give up the last bit of time with him, the last hours of pretending they were a couple, a family.

Chastened, she took her time putting the dishes away, and by the time she left the kitchen it was neater than she'd ever seen it before.

Devlin was sitting on the carpet in the middle of the big bedroom with a pajama-clad Sam and a book in his lap. Off to the side lay a scattered pile of empty yogurt cups, near the lopsided remains of a tower that had obviously collapsed of its own weight.

The scene was so powerfully domestic that Kady's eyes started to sting with tears of longing, and she paused in the shadowed doorway to get control of herself.

She thought she saw curiosity in Devlin's eyes, so she waved a hand at the failed construction project as if she'd been studying it and not the two of them. "Chartres Cathedral it isn't."

"No," Devlin agreed. "I don't think Sam's quite ready for the finer points of architecture. Of course, I don't think yogurt containers are likely to catch on as a serious building material, either."

Sam grinned and thumped the book.

"Maybe you should hope they do," Kady said. "At the rate Sam empties them, you could make a fortune. What are you reading to him?"

"The newest Crime Stompers."

"Comic books? You'll give him a complex."

"On the contrary. I'm introducing him to a marvelous heritage."

Kady stepped a little closer and looked over his shoulder. It was incredible, she thought, but when she looked at Devlin, his eyelashes appeared to be even longer and darker than usual. An artist would be fascinated with how the subdued light cut angles across his cheeks.... But of course she wasn't an artist. She was simply storing up the sight of him to keep her company on all the nights to come when she wouldn't be with him.

She pulled her gaze away from Devlin's face and forced herself to focus on the page. "He probably just likes the bright colors. Though actually these drawings are better than most comic book art. Not that I'm any judge, of course."

"As a matter of fact, you're right."

"That I'm no judge?" It was silly to feel just a little hurt—he was only agreeing with what she'd said herself.

"No, the illustrations are better." Devlin held up the book so she could look at it more closely. "One of the critics says the art is unusually clean and detailed."

"There are critics who specialize in comic books? Now I've heard everything." Kady turned the book at an angle so she could better study the drawings. "Not bad—but it's still beyond me to understand the fascination of these things. They don't even have a plot, and as for the glorification of bad guys—"

"On the contrary. The Crime Stompers are the good guys, and they'll always win in the end."

She handed the comic book back and sat on the carpet, pulling her knees against her chest and folding her arms around them. "There's still a lot of violence."

"Well," Devlin said reasonably, "you can't expect the hero to simply stroll up to the villain, politely ask him to mend his ways and get results. How long has it been since you've actually read a comic book, Kady?"

"I seem to remember sneaking one into my bed when I was about eleven, along with a flashlight so I could read it under the blankets in the middle of the night."

"They've changed since then," Devlin said dryly.

"I did it mostly because some of the boys thought the headmistress confiscated their copies because she was too cheap to buy her own, and I wanted to see what all the fuss was about."

"And?"

"I was terribly disappointed and never went back for more."

Devlin shook his head sadly. "You have no idea what you're missing. The modern comic book—"

"I still think it would be better for Sam if you'd read him something reasonable. Or don't you own anything but comic books? You could sing to him instead."

"The only song I know is 'The Twelve Days of Christmas.'"

Kady swallowed hard at the images that brought to mind, but she managed to keep her voice light. "Why not? He doesn't know the difference between Christmas and the Fourth of July."

But she did, and pictures of Christmas tumbled merrily through her mind—the kind of Christmas she'd only read about.

In six months, when the holiday arrived, Sam would be old enough to take delight in tinsel and wrapping paper and blinking lights on a tall pine tree. In six months, Devlin would probably be so comfortable in his role that the two of them would end up playing together. She could almost see Devlin crawling around to set up an electric train while Sam giggled and clapped his hands in delight.

And in six months, she told herself firmly, she would not be here to watch—so it was pointlessly cruel to torment herself with visions of things she would never see come to pass.

She took a deep breath and tried to distract her thoughts. "Why aren't you using the rocking chair, anyway?"

"It makes my elbows hurt. I'd rather spend the next six months sleeping in the desk chair in my study than use that rocker again."

Kady did her best to sound unsympathetic. "I told you to try it out before you bought it. I thought it was fine."

"Since you like it so well, I'll give it to you."

It was obviously no more than a careless comment. Still, the idea of a gift from Devlin made Kady's heart spin—and that fact made her furious with herself. It was ridiculous to let such a small gesture send her off the deep end.

Annoyance lent coolness to her voice. "As my Christmas bonus, you mean?"

Devlin didn't even pause to consider. "Oh, no. Christmas calls for something *really* special. I'll give you a full set of Crime Stompers."

Sam wriggled, grunted and grabbed for the comic book again.

"Sorry, Sam," Devlin said. "Kady won't admit the educational value of comic books, so I guess we'll have to wait for the next installment till she gets busy with something else." He started to hum.

Despite herself, Kady mentally filled in the words. *On the first day of Christmas, my true love gave to me...*

...A rocking chair, full of memory, she concluded. Any time she sat down in that piece of furniture, she would remember the warm, comforting weight of the baby in her arms, and also the cold, harsh burden in her heart because Devlin didn't—couldn't—care about her.

It was going to be difficult enough to put the memories of this weekend behind her. Having a reminder as concrete as the rocking chair was the last thing she needed.

"I imagine Tyler-Royale will take the chair back," she said coolly. "Just tell the customer service people it didn't work out the way you expected."

"It's certainly the truth," Devlin agreed. He began to sing.

Kady blinked in surprise. For a man with such a beautiful speaking voice, Devlin was hopeless at carrying a tune. If she hadn't known the words, she'd have had trouble identifying the song.

Sam tipped his head back till his neck nearly formed a right angle and stared into Devlin's face. Then he stretched out his left hand, laid his fingers across Devlin's mouth and grinned.

Kady tried, with minimal success, to choke back a laugh.

"I told you I wasn't much of a singer," Devlin pointed out. "Here—*you* entertain the pint-size critic."

She gathered Sam into her arms and sat in the rocker, matching the soft rhythm of the chair's movements with the gentle beat of a lullaby. Sam's eyelids grew heavy.

Devlin lounged on the carpet, leaning on one elbow and idly rebuilding Sam's yogurt-cup tower. When she finished the song and lapsed into silence, he said, "That was beautiful. Don't stop."

Kady was faintly embarrassed to discover he'd been listening. She'd assumed he was off in a world of private thought. "Sam's asleep."

"Well, I'm not."

"I hardly think you need a lullaby, Devlin."

He grinned. "So sing a little acid rock. I don't mind."

"I'm not a performer. I've had no training, so—"

"Never?"

"Well, who has time for voice lessons? And though we had a sort of chorus at Oakwood, it was a pretty informal exercise."

"That's a pity," he said softly. "Why don't you like scenes?"

Kady was startled. "What?"

"You told me this morning that you don't like scenes."

"Does anybody?"

"Actually, yes—or at least a lot of people seem to,

since they continually create them. Is it because of the school? There must have been an uproar going on all the time.''

Something about the way Devlin looked at her, the dark sincerity of his eyes, seemed to pull the truth from Kady. ''No, it wasn't Oakwood. I saw too many scenes before my mother died.''

The silence grew for what seemed eternity, and second thoughts crowded through Kady's mind. Why hadn't she done the simple thing and lobbed back the easy answer he'd so obviously expected? She certainly didn't intend to give him the details. He didn't need to know that her earliest memories were of the battles between her parents, or that her strongest recollections were from the time after her father had left, when other men had come and gone in her mother's life.

So why had she answered him at all? Perhaps it was his eyes—so dark, so intense, so watchful—that made it easy to convince herself he really wanted to know.

He wasn't making this whole weekend any easier on her, that was sure.

She stood up, cradling Sam in her arms, and walked across to the crib. The baby went down without a murmur, and she said softly, ''I think I did a better job of singing him to sleep than I really intended.'' She straightened and looked around the room. ''You know, Devlin, you might want to think about finding somewhere else to put his crib.''

The corner of Devlin's mouth quirked. ''Because someday I may want to go back to doing something besides sleeping in my bedroom, you mean?''

Annoyance sent Kady's common sense up in smoke, and before she'd stopped to think, the words were out. ''Well, I'd suggest you be a whole lot more careful in the future, or you're apt to have another Sam on your hands.''

Devlin's eyebrows soared. "And here I thought you considered him a darling," he drawled.

Kady already regretted letting the provocation get the better of her, but she could hardly back down now. After all, every word had been true. "The fact that he's cute is beside the point, don't you think? I mean, it's none of my business what you do, but—"

"It certainly isn't your affair. So why are you so concerned?"

She swallowed hard. *Because I care about you both,* she wanted to say. *And because I want you to care enough about me to turn your back on all the other women.* But that, of course, would get her precisely nowhere—except to a new high in embarrassment.

"I suppose I'm just nervous about Iris," she said. "I can't help but wonder how she'll take all this."

Devlin gave a little snort. "I wouldn't worry much about Iris. She's even less sensitive than an alligator's hide."

"Oh?" Kady said sweetly. "Is *that* where you acquired your immense levels of insight and compassion?"

"Bishop, somebody must have fed you razor blades in the nursery along with your formula," he grumbled.

"Well, obviously this line of conversation isn't likely to lead to anything positive." She faked a yawn. "So, since Sam's apt to be up at the crack of dawn again, I think I'll go to bed."

Too late, she realized that could be interpreted as an invitation. But Devlin was apparently oblivious—or uninterested. He merely nodded and vanished into the hall.

And I'm glad, Kady told herself as she stood in the middle of the bedroom and listened to the pounding of his footsteps down the staircase toward the kitchen. *That's a complication I certainly don't need.*

She shouldn't have snapped at him like that, though, about either his conduct or his grandmother. Not only did that kind of remark make her feel rotten about her lack of control, but it was dangerous.

Whatever Devlin seemed to think, sarcasm wasn't a normal part of her personality. It came out only when he was around—and that was where the danger lay. If he was to realize it was only him who could inspire that sharpness in her, then he might also be able to deduce the reason for it. And if once he discovered that Kady snapped at him because she was hurt—because though he didn't want her, she longed to be the only woman in his life...

That would be unbearable.

She had to stop sniping at him, that was sure. It was a sensible resolution, easy to make—though putting it into practice, she thought wearily, would probably be only slightly less difficult than achieving permanent world peace.

At least the picnic was behind them. Once they'd greeted Iris at the airport tomorrow afternoon, the last of the really tense moments would be over. If Iris took the news well, and if she wanted to get to know her new great grandson better, Kady could probably go about her own business right then.

Which brought her squarely back to the fact that she didn't want to do any such thing.

Part of her would feel relieved, of course, no matter when her tour of duty ended, because she'd no longer have to be on guard every moment. But the rest of her felt incredibly sad. Once the weekend was over, she'd never see Devlin and Sam in quite the same way again.

She'd still encounter them both, no doubt, whenever she returned to the town house to pay Devlin's bills and figure his payroll. Seeing them on such different terms wasn't going to be easy, but unless she dropped Devlin as a client, there would be no avoiding him.

She couldn't drop him, however, not only because she

couldn't afford to lose the business, but because she didn't want to encourage him to wonder about her reasons if she quit. So she'd have to continue her role as his accountant.

Perhaps she could manage to splinter a leg so badly she ended up in traction and couldn't manage the town house's stairs. At least that way she wouldn't have to see Sam—unless, of course, Devlin simply brought both the payroll and Sam to her hospital room. And why wouldn't he? He'd probably think she'd view the visit as a treat. He had no reason to think that seeing the baby would upset her. And since she wanted him to keep thinking that way...

With her brain revolving like a carnival ride, it took Kady a long time to fall asleep. Sam was perfectly still, apparently too exhausted from the fresh air and activity of the picnic even to roll over. The traffic outside seemed to have come to a standstill. And the town house was so quiet tonight that it was difficult for her to relax.

Kady had been used to noise all her life—the continual uproar of her home life followed by the sounds of the communal bedrooms at Oakwood, then the round-the-clock activity of a college dormitory and later the muffled noises of her apartment complex with its paper-thin walls.

She wondered what Devlin was doing that allowed him to be so quiet. She supposed he might not even be in the town house—though she couldn't imagine he'd have gone out without telling her.

And surely he wasn't sleeping in his desk chair again. The blankets he'd used last night were still on the bedroom floor, neatly folded in the corner, waiting for him....

She dreamed that he came to bed eventually and curled up beside her—and she roused to find herself clutching a pillow as if it had been him. From across the room she heard the soft whisper of a blanket sliding against the carpet, and she held her breath, half afraid there would be a repetition of last night—and half afraid there wouldn't.

She was being utterly hopeless, of course. It was past time to develop a little backbone where Devlin Cunningham was concerned. It wasn't as if she *wanted* him to hear her and know that she was awake and restless.

It was one thing to crave his touch. It was something else to invite it. She had no intention, she reminded herself, of being another of the less than memorable women who had occupied this bed.

That's it, she thought. *Instead of counting sheep to put myself back to sleep, I'll count the ladies who have slept here*!

And if Devlin appeared beside her and offered another neck rub, she'd just ask him bluntly if there was any woman in the world he could manage to keep his hands off. That would put him properly in his place.

His voice came out of the darkness, dry and level and not at all drowsy. ''Was that a serious question, or are you talking in your sleep?''

Kady felt as if tiny shards of ice had stuck in her throat, jabbing deeper each time she tried to take a breath. What was wrong with her, to have actually voiced her thoughts? And—maybe even more important—what exactly had she said?

Very deliberately, she gave a soft groan and followed it up with a murmur that she hoped sounded listless and lethargic enough to pass as the ramblings of an exhausted sleeper.

Devlin was silent.

Eventually Kady's tense muscles rebelled at staying still, and she turned over and buried her face in the pillow she'd been hugging. But just as she was beginning to relax again—convinced that whatever she'd said he had written off as half-conscious babbling—his voice broke the night again.

"Just in case you're playing possum," he said, so softly she had to strain to hear, "let me tell you this—it depends a whole lot on the woman."

Now that his brain was no longer so boggled over Sam, Devlin knew it shouldn't have been any surprise to find that Kady had moved in to absorb all his leftover reasoning power. The woman was either phenomenally innocent or the best little schemer he'd ever run into—and the damnable thing was, he still couldn't make up his mind which Kady Bishop was the real one.

Sometimes he believed she was as straightforward as she seemed. Take, for instance, those sensible cotton pajamas she was wearing tonight. The severe cut and the tiny floral print made the outfit look as if it had come straight out of Oakwood School's supply closet—and for all he knew, it had.

On the other hand, he had to admit, Kady Bishop in sensible cotton pajamas was a whole lot sexier than most cover models in black lingerie. The straight lines of sleeve and lapel formed a sensual contrast with the invitingly rounded curves of her body, which the soft fabric did nothing to hide. Did she really think she was less sexy wearing those pajamas than she had been in his royal blue satin boxers?

Didn't the woman realize how tempting she was?

Or did she know it very well indeed?

And, if she did, why had she closed off the discussion about Sam needing a mother? Because she honestly wasn't interested? Or because she was trying to raise the stakes?

The doorbell rang while Sam was pouring his bathwater from one side of the kitchen sink to the other with Devlin standing guard. Kady, who was supervising from a distance, saw Devlin wince at the sound of the Haydn *Surprise Symphony*. "I'll get it," she offered.

"Did you invite someone over?"

"Of course not. Why would I?"

Devlin shrugged. "Why not? It just occurred to me that you're dressed this morning for a change, so I thought you might be expecting someone."

At least he'd noticed that much, Kady thought wryly, though obviously it didn't matter a great deal to him whether she was fully clothed or not. "I only offered to answer the door because of pity for you. Since you look as if you're in pain from the sound, I thought I'd put a stop to it."

"Thoughtful of you."

"Yes, I am," Kady agreed. "However, now that I think about it, I seem to recall that the last time I answered the door it was Sam. So perhaps it would be better—"

Devlin's eyes brightened. "To ignore it?"

"To send you."

The bell rang again. "The first thing after the holiday, I'm getting rid of that tinny thing."

"Why?" Kady asked politely. "It's certainly an appropriate choice for a door that produces bombshells on the scale this one does."

She took her time on the stairs and glanced through the peephole before unlocking the door. All she could see, however, was a vaguely feminine shadow. The magnifying glass of the peephole was fogged, and the woman outside was standing at the edge of the tiny front porch, her back turned as if she was looking across the street—or trying to hide her face.

Cautiously, Kady opened the door. The woman turned, flashing a smile that didn't quite reach her eyes, and Kady blinked and looked again. *This*, she thought, *is Sam's mother.*

The woman was tall, slim and very blond. She wore a very short, tight red skirt and a matching loose-knit top with a designer silk scarf knotted skillfully at her throat, and the highest-heeled shoes Kady had ever seen.

Whatever had made this woman give up her baby, Kady thought, it didn't appear to be a lack of money—and she certainly had no shortage of style, either. Without even trying, she made Kady feel dowdy in her soft, worn jeans and comfortable T-shirt.

And without a doubt, she was Devlin's type.

The woman's smile hardened as Kady continued to stare blankly at her. "I'm looking for Devlin Cunningham," she said uncertainly. "I thought this was the right number, but—"

Astonishment flooded over Kady. Hadn't the woman even bothered to make sure where he lived before she'd dumped her baby?

Like water rushing into a too-small container, a primal urge to retaliate—to avenge Sam in some small way by punishing his mother—filled Kady's heart and overflowed. If she could make this woman feel just a little of the pain she'd inflicted on her son, perhaps she'd understand the horror of what she'd done.

Kady was still contemplating exactly how to do that when she saw the woman's eyes focus on something inside the town house. Her smile sprang to life once more.

Too late, Kady thought. *Sorry, Sam. It was probably hopeless, anyway.*

She could sense Devlin coming up behind her, as if he was radiating waves of warmth. "This...lady wants to speak to you, Devlin," she said levelly, without turning her head.

She didn't want to see his face when he got his first

good look at the woman outside. Whatever she saw there—whether it was surprise or distaste or renewed desire—Kady knew she wasn't apt to like it. But she couldn't hide from it, either. Sam's mother was a part of Devlin's life.

And you're not, Kady reminded herself. If seeing the way he reacted to this woman forced Kady to face reality, it would be worth the pain. So she forced herself to turn and watch him.

But Devlin didn't react at all. He looked calm—almost as if, Kady thought incredulously, the woman was no more than a casual acquaintance.

"I thought you'd be taking a long holiday weekend," he said.

The woman smiled. "And I thought *you* would. But I figured it was worth a try to catch you—just to show you how serious we are about this offer. May I come in?"

"My pleasure."

The woman stepped past Kady into the dimness of the hall. Her eyebrows climbed as she got her first good look at Sam, wrapped in a damp towel with his still-wet hair standing on end. "A baby? I'd never have thought it of you, Devlin."

Devlin looked at the child, quiet and watchful in his arms. "Oh, Sam just seemed more interesting than the usual Fourth of July fireworks," he said carelessly. "So I thought I'd give him a try this year."

Sam's face wrinkled. Obviously uncomfortable with being the sudden focus of attention, he whimpered and reached for Kady. She took him almost automatically.

"Kady, this is Jeannette Oliver from Constant Comics."

And I, Kady thought, *am a fool. Jumping to conclusions like that, just because a woman is young and blond and beautiful...*

Of course, even though Jeannette Oliver apparently wasn't Sam's mother, she was still Devlin's type.

Right, Kady told herself dryly. As if Devlin was so uncomplicated that only one kind of woman interested him!

The woman held out a hand. ''It's nice to meet you, Kady. What a beautiful baby you've got.''

Kady was still contemplating the possible answers to that comment when Jeannette Oliver slipped a hand into the bend of Devlin's arm. ''Can you give me a few minutes, Devlin? It's very important that we talk.'' She glanced around and drew him down the hall toward the offices.

For a woman who hadn't been certain of the house number, Kady thought wryly, Jeannette Oliver didn't hesitate to make herself at home. Kady suspected the woman wasn't seeking privacy so much as comfort. Kady would bet any amount of money Jeannette had already forgotten she and Sam even existed.

Kady closed the front door. She hoped, whatever was on Jeannette's mind, that it didn't take long. Iris Cunningham's plane was due to land in ninety minutes, and O'Hare was nearly an hour's drive away.

She took Sam upstairs, dressed him in the cutest outfit they'd bought and went downstairs to hover near the archway between hall and offices. She could hear the rise and fall of Jeannette's voice, but only occasionally the deeper tones of Devlin's. Even if she'd been trying, she couldn't have made out more than a word here and there.

Kady waited as long as she could, till the clock had ticked away the last uncommitted moments, and then strolled down the narrow aisle between cubicles till she saw Jeannette perched on the corner of Shelle Emerson's desk, toying with the knot in her scarf.

''It's not only been a success,'' Jeannette was saying,

"it's been the most impressive trial launch I've ever seen."

"The first issue sold out entirely," Devlin agreed, "and the second looks as if it'll do just as well."

Kady tuned out the talk. This was just another comic book that would be piled up in Devlin's storeroom within the next month or two. "Excuse me," she said. "But since I don't have my car, Devlin, I can't go meet Iris. And before you offer to loan me yours, let me remind you that I'm certainly not showing up at O'Hare with Sam in tow unless you go along. So you can either give me your keys and keep the baby, or else—"

Jeannette didn't seem to hear. "Now's the time to reach an agreement on future publication, Devlin." She leaned toward him with a confiding air. "My boss would kill me for telling you this, but he's eager to deal. He wants the Crime Stompers so bad he'll give you anything, because our lines have been dropping off in the last couple of years and we need new blood."

"And what's your price for helping to negotiate, Jeannette?"

She smiled and reached out to fiddle with his shirt collar. "Oh, I wouldn't put it that way at all. But if you happen to decide you need a personal assistant..."

Devlin stood up. "I'll think it over. Thanks for dropping by, Jeannette."

Kady leaned against the staircase rail and waited while he ushered Jeannette out. It took a while, and the woman was still talking when Devlin closed the door and, dusting his hands, came down the hall toward her. "Let's go. If traffic's light we can still make it in time."

"You'd better hope it is, or Iris will be standing at the baggage carousel breathing fire."

As if he was determined not to be left behind, Sam reached for Devlin, and Kady glanced into the diaper bag to be sure she'd remembered all the necessary supplies. "Devlin, what was that all about? Why are you involved in negotiating a sale for the Crime Stompers?"

"I'm not."

"It certainly sounded like it."

"And Jeannette would like to think so," he agreed. "But why should I sell out to her boss at Constant Comics? If I can have that kind of success with a new-title launch, why give up control now? Especially to someone who's been running a sinking ship for years?"

"*You* launched that series?"

He nodded.

"And you never told anybody?"

"What you really mean is, I never told you."

She had to admit he was right, but that didn't excuse him.

"And what would you have had to say about it if I had, Kady?" he went on. "Besides, of course, that it was a senseless investment, a waste of time and money..."

She might have said all those things, Kady knew, and with good reason—it had been a risky thing to do. But there was no sense in arguing about it now. "Speaking of money," she said, "where'd you get it? I mean, just as a matter of professional interest, how did you get those expenses past me?"

The doorbell rang again, and Kady glanced at her watch and winced. Even if they made every green light all the way to O'Hare, they were going to be late.

Devlin smiled. "So that ghastly tune is getting under your skin, too? It's probably just Jeannette."

"Coming back for something she forgot?"

"Or pretends to have forgotten," he agreed, and shifted Sam to the other shoulder.

"Well, she'll probably stand there all day if we don't answer." Kady flung the door open.

But the woman on the step wasn't Jeannette. She was

tiny and boyish, with a narrow triangular face and light brown hair caught up in a careless knot. Her enormous brown eyes flickered with interest when she saw Kady, but only for an instant. Then her gaze slid over Kady's shoulder and focused on something beyond.

Devlin, of course. Well, that was nothing new.

Then the woman spoke, in a surprisingly husky tone. "Sam! Oh, darling, Mommy's missed you so much!"

CHAPTER TEN

SAM'S face lit up as if someone had turned on a flashlight inside his brain, and his arms and legs churned madly until Devlin moved close enough for the baby to scramble out of his arms and into the woman's embrace. Sam's smile was so enormous that it stretched his face completely out of shape and showed dimples Kady had never dreamed existed.

Kady was still clinging to the doorknob. The woman standing on the porch was nothing like she'd expected Sam's mother to be. She was neither flashy nor hard-edged, and there was no mistaking the tears gleaming in her eyes as she snuggled the baby close.

But so what if she was suffering second thoughts, Kady told herself harshly. That didn't even begin to erase the fact that she'd abandoned Sam—dumped him like an unwanted puppy.

Kady wasn't sure who she was most irritated at—the woman who was cuddling Sam as if she intended never to put him down again, or Devlin, who was standing by grinning like an idiot, or even Sam, who was cooing and giggling....

Now that's completely irrational, she told herself. It was good that Sam felt loyalty and love for his mother. If the baby had transferred his affections to Kady and Devlin, it would only cause him pain if this woman reclaimed him.

Maybe, Kady admitted, she was most annoyed with

herself—for allowing a fantasy to root itself so deeply in her mind. For letting herself pretend, even though all the while she knew better, that in the end she might have Devlin and Sam to call her own.

Devlin's smile was almost as expansive as Sam's. Kady glanced at him once, briefly. The brilliance in his eyes hurt her as much as staring at the sun.

She knew it would hurt even more if she studied him closely enough to figure out exactly why he looked so delighted. In any case, it didn't matter to Kady whether he was so happy because Sam's mother was obviously going to take the baby off his hands, or because he was thrilled to see her again for his own sake. Neither alternative spoke particularly well of Devlin, and neither held any promise at all for Kady and that fantasy she'd cherished.

The knowledge that for her there would be no happy endings added an acid edge to her voice. "Perhaps you'd like to introduce us, Devlin?"

He shrugged. "I would if I could."

Kady was stunned. Surely he didn't mean that even when he was face-to-face with the mother of his child, he didn't recall her name! "What are you talking about?"

"I mean that I've never had the pleasure of meeting the lady myself, so how can I possibly introduce you?"

Kady blinked. "You don't know who she is? Now wait a minute. How—"

Devlin turned to the woman at the door and extended a hand. Sam, obviously thinking that Devlin was going to take him once more, frowned and shook his head firmly, then buried his face in the woman's shoulder.

The woman seized Devlin's hand. "You don't know how much I appreciate this. It was a lifesaver, really, and I'll never be able to thank you for letting me dump Sam on you.''

Well, Kady thought, at least she had a vague understanding of the enormity of what she'd done! "And you still say you don't know her, Devlin?'' she murmured.

"I can make an educated guess, but I'm afraid I don't know the name.''

The woman looked puzzled. "Devlin, I'm MaryBeth Mercer. We met at a party Iris gave last year.''

Last year? Kady thought in bewilderment. *But—*

Devlin nodded. "I knew you had to be one of her goddaughters, but I wasn't sure which one.''

"Well, of course I'm her goddaughter! You don't think I'd ask her to take care of my baby for a few days if I didn't know her? And then when she said she couldn't, but that you'd volunteered to take care of Sam—''

The room seemed to revolve around Kady, and everything took on a pale green hue. Her feet seemed to be nailed to the floor, which was a good thing, since the rest of her body was swaying like a stalk of grass in a strong breeze.

"You *knew*?'' Kady intended the question to come out firmly, accusingly, but it was only a whisper. "All the time, you knew?''

"No, I didn't.'' He turned to MaryBeth. "Iris didn't tell me I was baby-sitting, you see.''

MaryBeth looked as stunned as Kady felt.

"She just had Sam delivered,'' Devlin went on, with a tinge of irony in his voice, "sort of like a flower arrangement.''

After a moment, MaryBeth said, "But what on earth was she up to?''

"Who knows, with Iris? If I had to guess, I'd say she was hoping to shock me into reconsidering my life-style, and to prompt Kady into feeling warmly sympathetic about my problem.''

"Matchmaking?" MaryBeth said thoughtfully. "Well, that does sound a bit like Iris."

"*A bit*? Machiavelli himself would have run in horror if he'd met up with Iris!" The humor in Devlin's gaze as he met Kady's felt like salt water across sun-blistered skin.

So he found the whole idea funny, did he? she thought bitterly. He considered it a joke that Iris might think the two of them would make a compatible couple.

Too bad Kady didn't feel like laughing. She felt like a fool, instead.

It was a good thing Devlin didn't know the half of it, she reminded herself. *Warm sympathy* didn't begin to describe the emotional hurricane she'd been caught up in all weekend.

"By the way," Devlin went on thoughtfully, "he arrived complete with a note that implied I was his father."

"Well, don't look at me!" MaryBeth's voice was vehement. "*I* certainly wasn't involved in this—this scam."

"I didn't think you were."

"In fact," MaryBeth went on, "godmother or not, I'd like to punch her in the nose. To use my baby like that—"

Kady muttered, "Anybody who wants to punch Iris in the nose will have to get in line behind me." She thought she saw Devlin's gaze sharpen and added hastily, "I wasted a whole weekend over this stupid prank of hers, and Sam was miserable. When I get hold of Iris—"

"Now wait a minute, both of you," Devlin said peaceably. "Nobody got hurt. Sam was no more miserable here than he would have been anywhere else without his mother, and he's none the worse for wear."

MaryBeth hesitated as she studied the child nestled in her arms. "Well, no," she said reluctantly. "In fact, I'd say he's gained a couple of pounds and grown at least an inch."

Devlin nodded. "It must be all that yogurt Kady fed him."

Kady was no longer listening. What did Devlin mean, *nobody got hurt*? But of course, he didn't know how much this weekend—and he—had meant to Kady. He didn't know her heart felt like freshly ground hamburger.

And the last thing Kady wanted was for him to guess. She kept her voice taut. "Maybe we should all go meet her together and see what Iris has to say for herself."

Devlin grinned. "As a matter of fact, it might be fun to watch her face if we all marched in... Which reminds me, MaryBeth, was Iris expecting you to turn up today?"

MaryBeth shook her head. "We weren't supposed to be home till Wednesday, at least. My husband's being transferred to Houston, you see, so we went down to look for a house. But we found exactly what we wanted right away, so we did the paperwork and came on home."

Devlin nodded, obviously satisfied. "That explains why Iris changed her plans. I thought it was odd she wasn't around to watch me squirm."

"And now you're going to turn the tables on her?" MaryBeth grinned. "I guess I can give up the idea of personal revenge, then—as long as you promise to tell me all about it later. Now, if you'll point me to Sam's baggage, I'll get out of your way."

"I'll get his car seat," Devlin said, and vanished toward the garage.

"That's all he had," Kady said. "Just the seat and the clothes he was wearing. They're still in the laundry, I think."

"But when I dropped him off with Iris on Friday I brought everything he'd..." MaryBeth stopped. "Of course—she probably wanted him to look like an orphaned waif. What you must have thought of me! No wonder you stared at me the same way you'd eye an ax murderer."

"Sorry about that. Jumping to conclusions, I mean." Kady straightened a stack of comic books on the hall table. Her fingers were trembling, but it helped if she kept them busy.

MaryBeth stroked the baby's cheek. "I gather I have you to thank for the fact that Sam's reasonably happy?"

"I don't know about that. Devlin would have done all right, I think. And I wish," Kady added under her breath, "that I'd had the good sense to go away and let him try."

MaryBeth hesitated. "I'm sorry if all this mess has hurt your relationship with Devlin."

"What relationship?" Kady said drearily.

Devlin was back in minutes, and MaryBeth settled Sam into the seat and carried him out to her car.

Kady watched them go. She'd been sure her heart had already been blasted into oblivion, and yet when Sam—with his mother's prompting—waved goodbye, she felt as if one last shred was being ripped out of her chest. How quickly she had grown to love that little guy!

She was still staring out at the empty street when Devlin jingled his car keys beside her ear. "Are you ready? Iris is probably pacing the concourse by now, wondering what happened to us."

"She deserves to," Kady said. She didn't move.

"You're absolutely right. That's why I can't wait to

get there, to see what she says when we turn up without Sam. I think I'll tell her we left him chained in his play-pen. Or maybe that we just wrapped him in duct tape and—" He interrupted himself. "Come on, Kady. This is going to be a scene even you won't want to miss."

"She's probably taken a cab home by now—if she even went to the airport in the first place."

"What does that mean?"

"MaryBeth said she left Sam with Iris on Friday."

Devlin gave a low whistle. "So she wasn't in the Canary Islands at all?"

"At least not this weekend. She's probably been hiding out at home, feeding faxes to her friends overseas to make it look as if she was still halfway around the world."

"You sound a little disgusted, Kady."

"Any reason I shouldn't be? You could have told me what was going on, you know."

"And spoiled the fun? Just because Iris didn't let you in on all her secrets..."

Kady's head spun. She reached out for a stair rail to provide a little extra support and gritted her teeth. "You actually believe I was involved in this?"

"I thought you might be." Devlin's eyes were dark, almost somber. "I don't think so any more."

That was little comfort to Kady. "Let me get this straight. You think Iris and I schemed to set you up? Why would I—" She stopped. The reason was all too obvious. If Iris's plot succeeded in making Devlin reconsider his life, then the first woman who gave him sympathy might catch him on a sort of rebound. And who had been right at hand, ready to capitalize on the situation? "You're an egotistical blockhead, Devlin Cunningham!"

"For all I knew," he said soberly, "you were up to

your ears in this stunt. You were certainly willing to believe the worst of me—or at least you appeared to believe it. And you have to admit the timing of the whole thing looked pretty darned fishy.''

In a way, Kady couldn't blame him. Her mere presence in the town house at the moment Sam arrived must have looked awfully convenient. She even seemed to remember that before she'd answered the door on Friday, when the taxi had dropped Sam off, she'd tried to get Devlin to do it. It had probably looked as if she knew how important it was that he not ignore that summons.

No wonder he'd had his doubts.

But even a tinge of understanding didn't mute her fury. In fact, the knowledge that she'd so innocently played along made Kady angrier still. She had genuinely wanted precisely what he suspected her of scheming to get—Devlin himself. She'd been taken for a ride, not only by Iris's plot but by Devlin's failure to tell her what he knew—and that fact only added fuel to the fire.

If she'd been anything more to him than an amusing novelty, he'd have tried to work this out, to discover the truth about how deeply she was involved. But obviously he hadn't cared enough to investigate. He'd merely been amusing himself all along.

All right, she told herself. She didn't care, either, not really. It was enough to know that the man she'd fallen in love with—the softer side of Devlin Cunningham she thought she'd seen—had been only an illusion after all. That was all she needed. The details didn't matter.

Devlin's voice seemed to come from a great distance. ''I had only your story to go on,'' he said, ''and I knew how important you are to Iris, and how close to her.''

''So you thought I had to be involved in this.'' Kady congratulated herself on how casual she sounded.

''Well, anybody with the intelligence of—'' he

smiled. "—a dustpan would know I'd be more careful than to let a surprise like Sam creep up on me."

How dare he throw her own words back at her, with a laugh in his voice? Only sheer willpower kept Kady from seizing the first object she could reach and flinging it at him. Willpower, and also the last fragment of logic, which said that a stack of comic books was hardly the sort of weapon she'd have liked to throw at him. Now if there had been a nice crystal vase nearby, full of half-dead flowers and stagnant water...

"Have a good time agitating Iris," she said. "Do you mind if I use your phone to call a cab? No, on second thought, I'd rather try to hail one on the street."

She didn't wait for an answer. She tugged open the front door and walked out—away from the fantasy that had warmed her heart. Away from the man she loved.

That man was a phantom who existed only in her imagination, she told herself firmly. And since she was the one who had created that precious image, she could also destroy it. She could—she *would*—wipe Devlin Cunningham out of her mind.

Even if it took the rest of her life.

Kady had to go back, of course. She couldn't even write Devlin a simple letter terminating her contract as his accountant because she'd left her portable computer in his kitchen.

Not that she would resign, anyway, she told herself coolly on Friday afternoon as she parked her car in front of the town house. She was too professional to toss aside a paying client until she found a better account to replace him. And that was all Devlin represented to her now— a client, a payroll, a set of books, a stack of accounts payable.

She'd get through this first and most difficult encounter with her head held high. It would be difficult, but it wouldn't kill her.

She took half a dozen deep breaths before she rang the bell. It still played the Haydn *Surprise Symphony*, but she wasn't startled that Devlin hadn't gotten around to changing it yet. Though it felt like half a lifetime since she'd seen him, it had only been four days.

Hal opened the door and goggled at her. "Oh, it's you. I thought you'd have a key by now. I mean, after what I saw last weekend..."

Kady frowned with feigned concern. "What do you think you saw? Perhaps you should be more careful at these parties, Hal, if you're having delusions."

He scowled, but before he could answer Shelle Emerson came down the hall carrying a stack of comic books. She gave Kady an icy smile and said, to no one in particular, "How strange that some people can't use the back door like the rest of us do. Here, Kady—the third issue of the Crime Stompers is in. I just *knew* you couldn't wait to read it." She handed over a copy and set the rest of the stack on the hall table. "By the way, your computer is still downstairs. Whatever caused you to leave so suddenly that you forgot it?" She didn't wait for an answer before going toward her cubicle.

"Guess what!" Hal's scowl had cleared. "Speaking of the Crime Stompers, the boss is the one—"

"Who's creating it. I know."

Hal scratched his head. "How? He just told the rest of us at the noon staff meeting."

"You mean he was awake that early?" Kady knew the comment was unworthy of her, for Devlin hadn't exactly been a lie-abed over the weekend. Maybe he never had been, she thought, but had created the image on purpose simply to keep people like Kady from asking what he was really doing with his time.

Not that it mattered to her. The only important thing Hal had told her was what he didn't even know he'd said—that Devlin had been in the office an hour ago and was presumably still around.

Not that Kady would try to avoid him, even if she could. In fact, she almost wished Devlin would appear, just to get this first meeting over. This encounter would be the hardest. Once she'd faced him, it would never be quite so difficult again.

She wasn't afraid of what Devlin would do or say, exactly, for she didn't anticipate him making any kind of scene. Frankly, she expected he'd treat her as casually as ever—and that, she thought, would be more excruciatingly painful than any number of uncomfortable questions could be.

"Not only was I awake that early," Devlin said gently, "but I haven't gone back to bed since. Aren't you proud of me?"

Kady jumped at the sound of his voice and turned to face him.

He was standing on the stairway that led to his bedroom and study, one hand braced on the railing, the other tucked in his jeans pocket. He seemed to have grown taller in the four days since she'd seen him, for even discounting the height of the stairs, he loomed over her like an avenging warrior. And though his voice had held a faint note of irony, his eyes showed no trace of humor.

His gaze shifted from her face to Hal's. "Excuse us, will you, Hal? I need to talk to Kady."

"Sure, Devlin." But Hal paused in the doorway to add, "This discussion you're going to have won't delay the paychecks, will it? I've got a big weekend planned."

"It shouldn't take long," Devlin said dryly. "Come on up, Kady."

Kady felt a little breathless, and her heart ricocheted

like a Ping-Pong ball from her throat to her toes and back. In the six months she'd worked for him, she'd never heard anyone summoned upstairs into his private quarters for a business talk.

Devlin waited quietly for her to pass. Though the stairway was more than wide enough for both of them, Kady felt cramped, as if she had to shrink against the wall to avoid touching him.

Climbing the stairs, knowing he was only a step behind her, took incredible physical effort, and her muscles ached with the strain. The stillness—broken only by the murmur of office noises from the floor below and the sound of their footsteps on the wooden steps—was awkward. Afraid of the continuing quiet, Kady forced herself to speak. "Some things never change," she said.

"I beg your pardon?"

Kady realized belatedly that the statement could take on all sorts of meanings. "Hal's eagerness to get his paycheck, I mean."

Devlin didn't answer.

She tried not to glance into his bedroom, though the door stood wide open. From the hallway just outside the study, she could hardly avoid seeing the bedroom— the sunlight pouring through the wide windows, across the big bed, the expanse of carpet now innocent of toys and empty yogurt cups, the crib...

The crib? He'd left the crib?

She had no chance to wonder why. Devlin led the way into his study, shut the door, pointed to a chair and leaned against the corner of his desk. On the drawing table was a big sheet of paper, and on it, roughly sketched, was one of the characters she vaguely remembered from the comic book he'd been reading to Sam.

The room was filled with silence. She couldn't help remembering the night she had lain in the big bed in the next room, listening to that same quiet and feeling the same uncertainty. Only then—foolish as it had been— she had still nourished the conviction that everything would work out.

"You were right," Devlin said abruptly. "I should have told you what was going on."

Kady was staggered. Hope flared inside her like the flame of a just-struck match. If he'd used these last four days to reconsider... If he'd realized she would never have taken part in anything like his grandmother's scheme... If, perhaps, he had missed her...

She was still holding the comic book Shelle had handed her. Her fingers clenched, wrinkling the cover.

"After all," Devlin went on, "this is my business and I'm in charge—and it's my money I'm spending. So whether you think it's wisely spent or not isn't the point."

Kady's spirits dived like a crop duster.

When, she asked herself derisively, *are you going to learn that Devlin has never taken you seriously at all*?

"In fact," he said, "I intended to tell you last Friday, but you didn't seem to be in a mood to listen."

"*I* wasn't in a mood to...now that is downright unfair!"

"I didn't tell you before that because until I knew how the Crime Stompers idea was going to be received I didn't want to deal with questions—"

Kady interrupted. "And of course you thought I'd go straight to Iris."

Devlin went on as if she hadn't said a word. "Questions from you or Iris or anyone else who had no business asking them. But now I have some plans for capitalizing on the Crime Stompers' success, and I'm ready to talk about it."

Kady heard him detailing his ideas for a better quality

publishing process than most comics used, so the ink
would rub less and the drawings stay stronger. The prod-
uct would be more collectible that way, he said. The
distribution network he needed was already built, based
largely on his business in trading collectors' comics. If
all went well, before the year was out he'd be distrib-
uting for other small publishers as well as developing
another new series of his own. And he was starting to
look into the idea of publishing comics on compact discs
instead of paper....

He was all business, the entrepreneur talking to his
accountant—as if there had never been anything else between them.

And there hadn't, really, Kady thought. She felt too
sick inside over the way she'd deceived herself to really
concentrate, but the calculator in her brain was adding
up the costs nevertheless. The total would be astronom-
ical, and the business plan he'd mapped out sounded like
ten years of work compressed into two.

Before last week Kady would have argued with him
about the practicality of the whole idea. Now another
possibility occurred to her. Perhaps he was exaggerating
on purpose.

She interrupted. "Are you waiting for me to object so
you can fire me?"

Devlin's eyebrows went up. "Of course not. I'm going to need an accountant more than ever."

Kady would have given anything she possessed to be
able to tell him she didn't need his business. But that
would be a lie, both transparent and foolish.

Besides, she admitted, she didn't have the strength to
cut the ties. Each encounter would hurt—but it would
be worse never to see him again. She was like an addict,
longing for the one thing she knew might eventually
destroy her.

"It is your money, after all," she said. "As you've told me a dozen times."

"Good. I'm glad we agree on that much. I have the bills for the first two issues." He opened a desk drawer and pulled out a slim folder.

Kady flipped idly through the papers inside. There were statements from a printer, from a shipping company, from the advertising departments of a couple of magazines, and some of them were several months old. "Now at least I know how you kept me in the dark." She glanced at the rumpled comic book in her hand. "I never dreamed you were up to something like this."

"What did you think I was doing with all my time?"

Kady didn't answer, and Devlin didn't press the point. Perhaps, she thought, he didn't really want to hear what she would have said.

He sat on the corner of his desk and changed the subject. "Iris came over yesterday to apologize."

"Did she?" Kady kept her voice level, uninterested.

"She was quite contrite. She also said she'd tried a dozen times to call you, but she's only gotten your answering machine and you haven't phoned back."

Kady shrugged. "I've been busy."

"She even asked me what I thought she could do to make it up to you. I suggested you might like her to take a swan dive off the Sears Tower."

"Don't be ridiculous. She didn't mean it badly, I suppose—it just worked out that way. And Sam..." It made Kady want to cry just to think about that precious baby. "I'm glad I got to know him. Sam's a dear."

"Then you'll call her?"

Kady nodded.

The silence dragged out. But of course, there was nothing else to say.

"If that's all," Kady began, "I'll get started on the

payroll.'' Devlin made no objection, so she stood up. "By the way, I think it will be more efficient if I start working out of my office instead of coming here. Since I'll have less travel time, I can do a better job for you. Perhaps you can delegate someone to bring the paperwork over."

She was at the study door, her hand already on the knob.

Devlin hadn't moved, and he wasn't looking at her. "Kady, thanks for rescuing me this weekend."

His voice was as rich and warm as ever, but there was a note of finality in it. *All right*, Kady told herself, *be a good sport about it for two more minutes, and it will all be over. He'll never mention it again.*

She gave a little laugh. "Oh, you'd have managed. He's a great kid, easy to take care of." There was a catch in her voice, and she saw him look at her with something like curiosity in his eyes. Hastily, she added, "I miss him, you know."

Devlin looked away. "Obviously that's all you miss."

Kady stopped breathing. She was hearing things, she told herself. Or creating meanings once more that simply didn't exist because she wanted so badly to believe.

"And yet," Devlin said quietly, "today when you first saw me you jumped like a frightened rabbit. Why, Kady? What about me terrifies you so much that you don't want to see me again?"

"It's not that," she denied weakly. "I just think I could do a better job if I…"

Devlin had slid off the edge of the desk, and he was moving toward her like a panther stalking his prey. Slowly he raised his hands to cup her face, forcing her to look at him. "Is it this that frightens you?" He bent his head.

The brush of his palms made her skin ache with longing. "No," she whispered. "Don't."

"No, it doesn't frighten you? Or no, don't do that?"

Her body felt like jelly in an earthquake. She closed her eyes. *One last kiss*, she was thinking. *Just a sort of thank-you. That's all it means.*

And yet...

His lips against hers were cool and firm for just a moment. Then heat flared inside him. Kady could feel it scorching her skin, but she was too mesmerized even to try to pull away. The flame vaulted from him to her like wildfire leapfrogging through a forest, and she released a little moan and gave herself up to the sensation. He kissed her long and deeply, and she sagged against him.

Devlin's voice was rough. "It *isn't* just Sam you miss."

With her brain too shattered to consider the consequences, she told the truth. "No."

He held her even closer and laid his cheek against her hair. "You did a good job of hiding it. I thought the only thing that mattered to you was Sam—and your weekend's work, of course. So I kept trying to treat the whole thing as a joke, telling myself that being attracted to you was foolish, that I was only feeling drawn to you because we were cooped up together. Those pajamas of yours could make a corpse work up a good case of lust, you know. And for a normal, healthy man..."

She wasn't the only one who'd done a good job of hiding things, Kady thought.

"Then you went away," he went on softly, "before I was ready to let you go—and I couldn't forget. It wasn't till then that I knew it was more than just attraction. I love you, Kady."

Her body went rigid with shock.

Devlin's hold loosened, and he took a step back. "I

shouldn't have said that, I suppose. We spend a weekend in close quarters, and I declare I'm in love. It must look crazy.'' Irony almost dripped from his voice. "Or like a standard line.''

Kady couldn't help it—she nodded.

"And you certainly think I'm capable of that. But this didn't happen over the weekend, you know. It blindsided me—I never saw it coming. I must admit I wondered a few times why I didn't just fire you and find another accountant. Now I know. I must have started falling in love with you the first time you braced your feet and fought me.'' He shook his head. "Not that you care right now, do you? We got a bad start, with Iris's games, and Sam, and what you thought of me because of him. But I'm not giving up, Kady. If it takes the rest of my life, I'm going to convince you that there's too much going on between us not to give it a chance. When you kiss me like that—''

She swallowed the lump in her throat. "I care." It was all she could say.

He looked at her for a moment that seemed to stretch out into years. "You do?"

"I was scared," she admitted, eyes lowered. "Every ounce of logic said I was insane for being so attracted to you. You have to admit that you didn't exactly look like the poster boy for fidelity, Devlin.''

He smiled. "You do have a point there.''

"And when you wouldn't even admit that Sam might be yours—well, things like faithfulness and responsibility are important to me. Terribly important. Sometimes marriages don't work out, and I can understand that. But when someone turns his back on an innocent child—''

"Do you think I would, Kady?'' His voice was soft.

"No. Not now. But it all looked so clear then.''

"I wouldn't admit that Sam might be mine because I knew he wasn't."

"But how could you be so sure? I mean, you haven't exactly lived like a monk in the six months I've known you, so—"

"I've dated a lot of women, yes—but I'm not a specialist in one-night stands. Believe me, if I'd fathered a child, I'd have known it long before the kid was a year old."

Kady shook her head in disbelief. "I saw that list of women, Devlin."

"And you thought I'd slept with all of them? Oh, my dear—I was listing everybody I could think of who might have a reason to pull a con on me. Then Iris fired up the fax machine again, so I started looking up every godchild and protégé and friend and pal of hers—"

"Why?"

"I was trying to find somebody who'd recognize Sam."

"But why were you so sure Iris was behind this?"

"Because each of us got a fax. Of course she'd send two, trying to throw off my suspicions. Believe me, I know how her cunning mind works."

Kady shook her head. "I still don't see it."

"Well," he said generously, "I had the benefit of knowing that no one could have sprung a baby on me for real. So it was just a question of finding out who'd engineered it—and Iris was suddenly showing a lot of interest in what I was up to."

"One fax is a lot of interest?" Kady said doubtfully.

"For Iris, yes. And don't forget she'd arranged it so I had to go to the picnic, and asked you to get me there and the headmistress to check up on me. It was too much."

"Well...maybe."

"I was right, wasn't I?"

She couldn't argue with that. "Is that why you sort of relaxed about then and started to enjoy Sam? Because you'd figured out what was going on?"

He nodded. "I could see the rough edges of the plot, anyway."

"I thought you'd decided fatherhood was inevitable, so you might as well give in."

"No. Thinking about you was inevitable, though. When Sam first arrived, I was genuinely panic-stricken—I'd never been around a kid that age before, and I was terrified he'd break. Then I saw the benefits of keeping you where I could watch you, just in case you were in on the scheme."

"You have a nasty, suspicious mind, Cunningham."

"No doubt it's because I spent too much time with Iris when I was a kid. But eventually I realized that wanting you to stay had nothing to do with Sam, and everything to do with me."

The warmth in his voice spread comfortingly through Kady's body, relaxing each tense muscle. And the way he was holding her, confidently, easily, as if he intended never to let go, made her bones start to melt.

"Of course," he said thoughtfully, "you didn't seem to feel anything of the sort. When I suggested you'd be a good mother, I might as well have announced that I had leprosy. You couldn't have reacted any more strongly."

"I was afraid, Devlin." She bit her lip and told him what she had never said to anyone before. "All my life I've been the one nobody really wanted. The leftover. And I was afraid that if you wanted me at all it was only to make your life easier where Sam was concerned."

Though Kady would have said it wasn't possible, he held her even closer. She thought wryly that the imprint of the buttons on his shirt would probably be a permanent part of her—the sort of tattoo she would treasure forever.

"No," he said firmly. "And you're not a leftover now, Kady. I promise you will never be unwanted again."

She sighed and put her head on his shoulder, feeling more at home in his arms than in any place she'd ever lived.

It was a long time later when they went downstairs and found Shelle in the hallway, her hand on the banister as if she was starting to climb the steps. "Hal's beginning to pace the floor and mutter about his paycheck," she said.

"I'll take care of it right now," Kady said, and started to pull away.

Devlin caught her hand and drew her back to his side. "Let him pace."

Shelle's eyes sharpened. "Well, well, well," she said. "Isn't that interesting? Where's the kid today, anyway?"

"Oh, we don't have him any more," Devlin murmured. "We exchanged him at Neiman-Marcus for a gift certificate."

"Yeah, right." Shelle tossed her hair and stalked into the office.

"Something tells me I've lost all credibility where Shelle is concerned, and she'll no doubt be looking for another job soon." Devlin nibbled at Kady's earlobe. "I wonder what she'd have said if I'd told her Sam was second prize in one of those sweepstakes offers that are always coming in the mail."

"*Second* prize?"

"Of course. Sometimes in those things you have to

turn down one award to have the chance of winning a better one. And I was lucky enough to win the grand prize.''

His kiss left Kady in no doubt about who he meant. Sheer happiness caught at her throat, leaving her unable to speak—so she answered him the only way she could. Eventually, however, she tried to pull herself back to reality. "Devlin, we're standing in the hallway."

He sounded only mildly interested. "Why does that bother you? It's level, warm, quiet—"

"Well, there *are* half a dozen employees in the next room."

"I'm not trying to keep any secrets. Baby, you're mine—and the sooner everybody knows it, the better I'll feel."

He drew her close again, and Kady forgot about the possibility of an audience in the sheer joy of being in his arms.

"I think," he said finally, "that we should buy Sam a really wonderful thank-you gift."

"Like a loving cup or something? I miss him, Devlin."

"Me, too. He was a lot of fun."

"Maybe we can borrow him again someday."

"Why not? We've already got all the equipment...." He paused to kiss her again, long and passionately, and it was a full two minutes later before he went on, his voice unsteady. "Though a part-time kid might not be enough to satisfy us. Maybe we should consider a Sam of our own, instead."

Kady gave a long and contented sigh. "Convince me," she said.

Devlin's smile was half lazy sensuality and half wickedness. "Now that," he murmured, "sounds like the kind of challenge I'd enjoy.''

The Fourth of July was past, of course. But their own, very private fireworks were the most satisfying of all.

EVER HAD ONE OF THOSE DAYS?

TO DO:

☑ late for a super-important meeting, you discover the cat has eaten your panty hose

☑ while you work through lunch, the rest of the gang goes out and finds a one-hour, once-in-a-lifetime 90% off sale at the most exclusive store in town (Oh, and they also get to meet Brad Pitt who's filming a movie across the street.)

☑ you discover that your intimate phone call with your boyfriend was on company-wide intercom

☑ finally at the end of a long and exasperating day, you escape from it all with an entertaining, humorous and always romantic Love & Laughter book!

ENJOY
LOVE & LAUGHTER™
EVERY DAY!

For a preview, turn the page....

———————————

"DARLING, YOU SOUND like a broken cappuccino machine," murmured Charlotte, her voice oozing disapproval.

Russell juggled the receiver while attempting to sit up in bed, but couldn't. If he *sounded* like a wreck over the phone, he could only imagine what he looked like.

"What mischief did you and your friends get into at your bachelor's party last night?" she continued.

She always had a way of saying "your friends" as though they were a pack of degenerate water buffalo. Professors deserved to be several notches higher up on the food chain, he thought. Which he would have said if his tongue wasn't swollen to twice its size.

"You didn't do anything...bad...did you, Russell?"

"Bad." His laugh came out like a bark.

"Bad as in *naughty*."

He heard her piqued tone but knew she'd never admit to such a base emotion as jealousy. Charlotte Maday, the woman he was to wed in a week, came from a family who bled blue. Exhibiting raw emotion was akin to burping in public.

After agreeing to be at her parents' pool party by

noon, he untangled himself from the bed sheets and stumbled to the bathroom.

"Pool party," he reminded himself. He'd put on his best front and accommodate Char's request. Make the family rounds, exchange a few pleasantries, play the role she liked best: the erudite, cultured English literature professor. After fulfilling his duties, he'd slink into some lawn chair, preferably one in the shade, and nurse his hangover.

He tossed back a few aspirin and splashed cold water on his face. Grappling for a towel, he squinted into the mirror.

Then he jerked upright and stared at his reflection, blinking back drops of water. "Good Lord. They stuck me in a wind tunnel."

His hair, usually neatly parted and combed, sprang from his head as though he'd been struck by lightning. "Can too many Wild Turkeys do that?" he asked himself as he stared with horror at his reflection.

Something caught his eye in the mirror. Russell's gaze dropped.

"What in the—"

Over his pectoral muscle was a small patch of white. A bandage. Gingerly, he pulled it off.

Underneath, on his skin, was not a wound but a small, neat drawing.

"A red heart?" His voice cracked on the word *heart*. Something—a word?—was scrawled across it.

"Good Lord," he croaked. "I got a tattoo. A heart tattoo with the name Liz on it."

Not Charlotte. Liz!

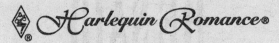

Harlequin Romance®

is proud to announce the latest arrivals
in our bouncing baby series

BABY BOOM

Each month in 1997 we'll be bringing you your very
own bundle of joy—a cute, delightful romance by
one of your favorite authors. Our heroes and heroines
are about to discover that two's company and three
(or four...or five) is a family!

Find out about the true labor of love...

Don't miss these charming stories
of parenthood, and how to survive it,
coming in May, June and July.

**May—THE SECRET BABY (#3457)
by Day Leclaire
June—FOR BABY'S SAKE (#3461)
by Val Daniels
July—BABY, YOU'RE MINE! (#3463)
by Leigh Michaels**

Available wherever Harlequin books are sold.

HE SAID

♥

SHE SAID

Explore the mystery of male/female communication in this extraordinary new book from two of your favorite Harlequin authors.

Jasmine Cresswell and Margaret St. George bring you the exciting story of two romantic adversaries—each from their own point of view!

DEV'S STORY. CATHY'S STORY.
As he sees it. As she sees it.
Both sides of the story!

The heat is definitely on, and these two can't stay out of the kitchen!

Don't miss **HE SAID, SHE SAID.**
Available in July wherever Harlequin books are sold.

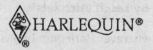

HARLEQUIN®

Let's Celebrate!

LOVE & LAUGHTER™

invites you to the party of the season!

Grab your popcorn and be prepared to laugh as we celebrate with **LOVE & LAUGHTER**.

Harlequin's newest series is going Hollywood!

Let us make you laugh with three months of terrific books, authors and romance, plus a chance to win a FREE 15-copy video collection of the best romantic comedies ever made.

For more details look in the back pages of any Love & Laughter title, from July to September, at your favorite retail outlet.

Don't forget the popcorn!

Available wherever
Harlequin books are sold.

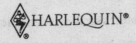

◆HARLEQUIN®

Look us up on-line at: http://www.romance.net   LLCELEB

New York Times Bestselling Authors

JENNIFER BLAKE
JANET DAILEY
ELIZABETH GAGE

Three *New York Times* bestselling authors bring you three very sensuous, contemporary love stories—all centered around one magical night!

It is a warm, spring night and masquerading as legendary lovers, the elite of New Orleans society have come to celebrate the twenty-fifth anniversary of the Duchaise masquerade ball. But amidst the beauty, music and revelry, some of the world's most legendary lovers are in trouble....

Come midnight at this year's Duchaise ball, passion and scandal will be...

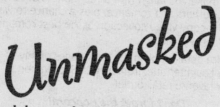

Unmasked

Revealed at your favorite retail outlet in July 1997.

FORTUNE COOKIE

Breathtaking romance is predicted in your future with Harlequin's newest collection: Fortune Cookie.

Three of your favorite Harlequin authors, Janice Kaiser, Margaret St. George and M.J. Rodgers will regale you with the romantic adventures of three heroines who are promised fame, fortune, danger and intrigue when they crack open their fortune cookies on a fateful night at a Chinese restaurant.

Join in the adventure with your own personalized fortune, inserted in every book!

Don't miss this exciting new collection!

Available in September wherever Harlequin books are sold.

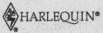

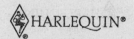

HARLEQUIN AND SILHOUETTE
ARE PLEASED TO PRESENT

Love, marriage—and the pursuit of family!

Check your retail shelves for these upcoming titles:

July 1997
Last Chance Cafe by Curtiss Ann Matlock
The most determined bachelor in Oklahoma is in trouble! A
lovely widow with three daughters has moved next door—and
the girls want a dad! But he wants to know if their mom needs
a husband....

August 1997
Thorne's Wife by Joan Hohl
Pennsylvania. It was only to be a marriage of convenience—
until they fell in love! Now, three years later, tragedy
threatens to separate them forever and Valerie wants only to
be in the strength of her husband's arms. For she has some
very special news for the expectant father...

September 1997
Desperate Measures by Paula Detmer Riggs
New Mexico judge Amanda Wainwright's daughter has been
kidnapped, and the price of her freedom is a verdict in
favor of a notorious crime boss. So enters ex-FBI agent
Devlin Buchanan—ruthless, unstoppable—and soon there is
no risk he will not take for her.

If you are looking for more titles by

LEIGH MICHAELS

Don't miss these fabulous stories by one of
Harlequin's most popular authors:

Harlequin Romance®

#03248	SAFE IN MY HEART	$2.89	☐
#03263	TIES THAT BLIND	$2.89	☐
#03300	A SINGULAR HONEYMOON	$2.99	☐
#03343	HOUSE OF DREAMS	$2.99 U.S.	☐
		$3.50 CAN.	☐
#03367	TAMING A TYCOON	$2.99 U.S.	☐
		$3.50 CAN.	☐
#03411	THE DADDY TRAP	$3.25 U.S.	☐
		$3.75 CAN.	☐
#03423	MARRYING THE BOSS!	$3.25 U.S.	☐
		$3.75 CAN.	☐
#03444	THE PERFECT DIVORCE	$3.25 U.S.	☐
		$3.75 CAN.	☐

(limited quantities available on certain titles)

TOTAL AMOUNT	$	
POSTAGE & HANDLING	$	
($1.00 for one book, 50¢ for each additional)		
APPLICABLE TAXES*	$_____	
TOTAL PAYABLE	$_____	

(check or money order—please do not send cash)

To order, complete this form and send it, along with a check or money order
for the total above, payable to Harlequin Books, to: **In the U.S.:** 3010 Walden
Avenue, P.O. Box 9047, Buffalo, NY 14269-9047; **In Canada:** P.O. Box 613,
Fort Erie, Ontario, L2A 5X3.

Name: _____

Address: _____ City: _____

State/Prov.: _____ Zip/Postal Code: _____

*New York residents remit applicable sales taxes.
Canadian residents remit applicable GST and provincial taxes.   HLMBACK8

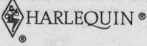

HARLEQUIN ®

Look us up on-line at: http://www.romance.net